"TOTALLY INELIGIBLE! HE IS TYRANNICAL, OVERBEARING, AND WITHOUT GRACE OR MANNERS! WHAT IS MORE, HE IS ENGAGED TO ANOTHER FEMALE."

—Theodosia's Opinion of Viscount Claremont

Also by Rebecca Baldwin:

THE CASSANDRA KNOT

A GENTLEMAN FROM PHILADELPHIA

THE MATCHMAKERS

PEERLESS THEODOSIA

A Regency Love Story by

Rebecca Baldwin

FAWCETT COVENTRY • NEW YORK

PEERLESS THEODOSIA

Published by Fawcett Coventry Books, a unit of CBS Pub-
lications, the Consumer Publishing Division of CBS Inc.

ISBN: 0-449-50036-5

Printed in the United States of America

First Fawcett Coventry printing: March 1980

10 9 8 7 6 5 4 3 2 1

For JAMES SINDERMANN,
One Third of the Bentfin
Boomer Boys Plus The Lady
Writer

CHAPTER ONE

The Venetian clock on the morning-room mantelpiece chimed softly on the quarter hour.

Lady Southcote, a deceptively delicate-looking matron of forty-odd summers, dressed very becomingly in a morning dress of gage-green merino with the smallest ruff framing her face, pulled her Paisley shawl closer about her shoulders and stood back from the table to study the flower arrangement she had been working on. Absently tapping the head of a Queen Anne rose against her hand, she narrowed her eyes. While she was able to feel a great deal of satisfaction in knowing that Southcote Place had the best series of greenhouses in Devon, she could not but feel regret that winter roses lacked the size and color of those grown in the summer.

Lady Southcote was a vigilant and skillful horticulturist. At least one hostess had ordered an entire border of gloxinias ripped out of her gardens upon Lady Southcote's dry "Very interesting!"

Still, she thought, glancing out the window at the cold, gray landscape, one could wish that November were not such an unproductive month, such a dead month in the country.

All about Her Ladyship, Southcote Place was functioning as smoothly as her Venetian clock. In the west-wing schoolroom, her youngest children, known in the family as Hessie and Gussie, were bent over their schoolbooks under the cold eye of Miss Rowenna Ipstone. In the library, Lady Cynthia Southcote was engaged in a letter to her friend Mrs. Palmer, now a married lady in the Midlands; Gibney, the formidable butler, was polishing the silver in the pantry, regaling the second footman with a strong lecture on the proper service of luncheon at a gentleman's country estate; in the forcing houses, MacKeague, the head gardener, was spraying a tincture over the trees in the orangery to prevent winter blight. And all through the house and grounds, a small army of servants were moving through their daily chores. Lady Southcote prided herself on a well-run household.

With a small sigh, she moved the vase to the center of the table. While she loved the country, she was finding this forced confinement in the midst of the Season deadly dull. But what was a concerned mother to do when both of her youngest twins came down with influenza at the same time? Country air, Dr. Baillie had said firmly, was the best cure; at least three months of it. Lady Southcote hoped she was not an unnatural mother, but after a very few weeks it had seemed to her that Hester and Augustus had not only made a total recovery, but were even more lively than before, if possible, always into some new mischief. And Cynthia, deprived of the entertainments that a young lady in her second Season should be indulging in, seemed to be even more bookish than ever, without the stimulation of London life and friends of her own age.

Lady Southcote thrust the last rose into the center of

the vase and pulled out another. Three months, Dr. Baillie had said, and three months it would be. Frowning, she wondered how it could be that her eldest daughter could be both so beautiful and so bookish. She had begun to fear that no gentleman would offer for a female who made so little attempt to disguise her intelligence, even a female with the face and form of her daughter.

Not that Lady Southcote liked missish females. If Cynthia had grown up to be a simpering miss with die-away airs, she would have been even more seriously disturbed. If only the Marquess had—

Lady Southcote was so absorbed in her thoughts that she did not hear the rumble of carriage wheels on the drive or glance up to catch a glimpse of a handsome barouche and two scarlet-coated outriders drawing up to the door.

She started when the door of the morning room opened to admit a tall, white-haired man dressed in somber black, who threw his case and gloves carelessly on the table. "I swear that butler you've got doesn't recognize me, Henriette!" this gentleman exclaimed, gathering Lady Southcote into a brief embrace.

"Charles!" she murmured, considerably taken aback. "I thought you were in Vienna!"

The Earl of Southcote was a very tall man, and he had to bend over to kiss his wife's pink cheek. Releasing her, he strode to the fireplace and seated himself in his favorite chair, propping his gleaming boots against the grate. "I *was* in Vienna, my love, but I was called back. Tomorrow, I'm off to Ghent. The Americans are getting ready to negotiate a treaty. I've only got a few hours, my love, so you must forgive my coming so unexpectedly. It's better if it's not generally known I was in the country—yet."

From an interior pocket, the earl withdrew a silver snuff box and inhaled deeply, watching his spouse over his cuff. "Dashed fetching gown, Henriette. Green always did become you."

Lady Southcote permitted herself a smile and seated herself opposite her husband.

Through nearly thirty years of marriage, she had resigned herself to the idea that the diplomatic service was her husband's mistress. And if she had no head for the complications of foreign intrigue and privately deplored the earl's lack of interest in the domestic affairs of his family and estate, she was comforted by the fact that his position in the government, his reputation as a statesman, and his rank gave her and her children a great deal of consequence in the world.

Nearing the half-century mark, the earl showed few signs of slowing down. True, his hair was snow white, swept back from an ever-higher forehead, and the lines from the corners of his mouth to the edges of his long thin nose were deeper. But his black eyes were as piercing as ever, and the set of his jaw betrayed no weakness.

"I see I still find you in the country, Henriette. I was somewhat surprised when I arrived in London and found the house closed up. But no matter, I believe this will suit my purposes even better than I had expected."

Lady Southcote folded her hands patiently. "You must recall that Hessie and Gussie came down with the influenza, Charles, right before you left for Vienna."

His Lordship's brows went up slightly. "Oh, of

course, of course. It *had* slipped my mind, you know. About that time Melbourne was—well, never mind. And I trust that Cynthia is well?"

"She *reads* a great deal," Lady Southcote said doubtfully. "I fear the country is not providing her with enough stimulation."

"The Marquess didn't come up to scratch, then?" Lord Southcote asked shrewdly.

His wife shook her head sadly. "I had hopes—but Cynthia gave him so little encouragement, poor man. I fear she thinks him rather frivolous."

"Friv—" The earl snorted. "Steyland's one of the prime catches of the *ton*. When he takes his seat—well, I could use a son-in-law in the House! Lord, Henriette, what sort of a daughter did you raise?"

"One too much like her father, I fear," Lady Southcote said calmly, quite used to these accusations. "I trust you saw Clare when you were in London?"

At that moment, Gibney entered the room, bearing a tray of Madeira and cold luncheon. "The footman you dispatched to Honiton with your message is on his way, my lord," he said majestically, removing himself as silently as he had come.

The earl helped himself generously to the Madeira. "Thing of it is, Henriette—"

"Clare," she reminded him patiently. "Your oldest son."

Southcote raised one brow. "I know who my son is, dash it, Henriette. And he's as gloomy as his sister. Oh, nothing you can put your finger on, you know; Hemphill says he's doing well in the Foreign Office, and he's at his clubs, and at Jackson's but—" The earl shook his head doubtfully. "No spirit in him, I fear. He's as quiet as a Quaker, and just as serious!"

"And he has been, ever since poor Guy died in Spain," her ladyship said sadly, thinking of her dead son with regret. "Guy, you know, could always cheer him out of his megrims, and he could always restrain Guy from his excesses, but now . . . " She broke off thoughtfully. "You know, I read something the other day, in a novel, I think, about the mystical bond between twins. I believe that Guy's death quite knocked the life out of Clare. . . ."

"More likely that chit he's engaged to. Dull dish, that one, always prosing on in the deadest fashion. All the Morton-Wests are like that, and always have been. Wouldn't be surprised if that's where Cynthia gets her bluestocking ideas from!" The earl helped himself to cold beef.

Lady Southcote, understanding these references to Claremont Southcote's fiancée, Miss Edwina Morton-West, shook her head. "Oh, no! Cynthia is quite—that is—well, she does not feel entirely comfortable with Edwina. Edwina, she says, is completely given over to vanity and hypocrisy."

"Does she, now?" the earl said, with something close to approval in his voice. "Well, between you and me, Henriette, I don't see what Clare sees in that female. She's cold as ice, that one; not at all the sort of wife one would wish for a diplomat. Complete opposite of you, my dear."

"Thank you, Charles," Her Ladyship said serenely. "I trust that I have always acted with your interests in mind." She twisted the fringes of her scarf through her fingers. "But Clare does worry me, sometimes. He acts quite normally, and he is a good son and brother, but it is as if some part of him were laid in the grave with poor Guy."

The earl was not a romantic. He merely shrugged. "He'll get over it, I suppose, as he advances in the Office. Hang it, Guy's been gone these two years, pretty near. Anyway, it's not our children I'm worried about, right now. It's Thaddeus Clement's!"

Lady Southcote searched her memory and nodded. "Oh, yes, the American—what do you call it—Senator? The gentleman we met in Paris, during the Peace? You were at Oxford together, was it?"

"Exactly." The earl nodded. "Knew I could count on you not to forget a face! Clement's in Ghent now—he's been consul in Milan for several years, getting mixed up with the Bonaparte crew, no doubt. And, knowing him, I'd be hard put to tell who had the short end of that! But never mind. The thing is, Clement's children are in England."

"England!" Lady Southcote was at sea. "But we are at war with America, are we not? How could two American children come to be in England?"

Her husband piled slices of cold ham on a piece of bread. "Through an incredible piece of bungling in the Admiralty! If it weren't for the bungling of some overzealous young captain, right now they would be in Milan, where they belong, instead of being put up at the Admiral Bowditch in Plymouth! Causing Lord only knows how much embarrassment to the Office! It seems they were on an Italian ship, bound for New York—under a neutral flag, mind you!—when this bungling captain gets it into his head to stop and search the ship. Felt it was his duty to take the two Americans

13

on board into custody! I can't tell you what a flap there was about that! Clement's the man to bring about a peace, and here are his children being held prisoners of war in England! A grand tangle, let me assure you, Henriette! How does it look when I go to Ghent and inform one of my oldest friends that his children are prisoners of war in my country? Liable to set back the peace for months!" The earl looked at his wife from under his brows. "How would you feel if our children were held in some inn in Washington! It's a terrible tangle!"

Lady Southcote's kind heart was touched by the vision of two children, alone and friendless in an alien country. Mr. Clement she remembered to be a very nice gentleman who knew a great deal about the training of privet hedges. He had sent her some particularly lovely cuttings of a wild American rose. The thought of his children, motherless as they must be, for now she recalled he was a widower, confined to an inn in a rough seaport city made her bosom swell with indignation.

"Charles, you must use all of your influence to have them delivered here instantly!" Clutching her shawl against her breast, Lady Southcote looked up at her husband, her face alight with passion. "Oh, the poor dears! What a terrible ordeal for them, with those rough sailors in Plymouth, kidnapped off the high seas! Charles, do not hesitate, they must be brought to me at once, those poor motherless creatures!"

The earl smiled down at his spouse. "I knew you'd agree to it, once you heard the story, Henriette! Then I'll have it set all right and tight! I knew you'd be willing to smooth things over, once you understood, my love, just how things were."

"I should hope so!" Lady Southcote replied. "Could you really think that I would be so devoid of feeling as to leave two children alone and friendless in a strange country? What possible threat can two children pose to the security of England? Men, I swear!" She dabbed at the corners of her eyes with her shawl.

Lord Southcote patted his spouse's shoulder. "You're pluck to the backbone, Henriette!" he said bracingly. "I knew that you'd come through, once you understood just how it is."

"Mama, what does this mean? Papa, I knew you must be here!"

Cynthia Southcote stood in the doorway, holding a book in one hand, as she looked anxiously at her father. At seventeen, she had just come into the first bloom of her beauty. Her skin was the tone of alabaster, tinged with the faintest blush of rose; a slender nose sloped down her heart-shaped face above delicate red lips, while her eyes, the color of a Devon sky, were fringed with thick brown lashes, framed by perfectly curving brows. A profusion of flaxen curls escaped from a pink riband wound loosely through her hair. Like her father, she was tall and graceful. A simple round gown of pink muslin, caught at the roll of the sleeves and the hem with small love-knots of white silk braid, set off her face and figure to perfection. Yet she seemed sublimely unconscious of her good fortune, for, as she walked across the room to kiss her father, she pulled the riband away from her hair and held it in her hand.

Lord Southcote, never overinterested in the style and

features of his offspring, found himself caught by her resemblance to her mother at the same age.

"Well, Cynthia, I trust I find you well?" he asked, smiling vaguely at her.

His eldest daughter nodded. "Yes, Papa," she said meekly. "We did not expect you back from Vienna until after Christmas, you know."

"And so you didn't. I've just come to tell your mama that the Admiralty's gotten itself in a tangle that she'll have to get us out of. But I'll let her explain it all to you, for I'm off to Plymouth, and then Ghent, within the hour."

Cynthia nodded. "I see, Papa. But I hope you don't mean for Mama to have another one of those balls for the uniforms—"

Lord Southcote frowned slightly. "I never met a young lady yet who didn't like a ball. Is something the matter, Cynnie?"

Lady Cynthia glanced at her mother and bit her lip. "No, Papa. Nothing. I'm sorry you can't stay," she added wistfully, twisting the riband around in her hands.

Lord Southcote patted her shoulder absently, glancing at his watch. "Be back after Christmas sometime. Don't quite know when the Americans will come up to snuff. I daresay you're in the megrims, being stuck out here in the country in the midst of the Season?"

Cynthia shook her head. "No, not really. I could not be so selfish as to want to be partying while Mama and Miss Ipstone were worn into a frazzle about the twins. I find the country very quiet, and very restful."

"Good girl!" Lord Southcote murmured. "See that you take care of your mother, now, and your new visitors. Should you like it if I bring you back a bauble from Ghent?"

She smiled. "Oh, yes, Papa, that would be very nice. But Papa, I would like to talk to you before you—" Cynthia's expression was anxious, as if it took a great deal of courage to force the words out. Unfortunately, she never finished the sentence, for at that moment the room was filled with two small tornadoes who seemed to be everywhere at once as they called for their Papa.

Hester and Augustus, having escaped from Miss Ipstone's watchful eye, flung themselves joyously upon their startled father. "Papa! What did you bring us from Vienna?" they exclaimed in unison, each one grasping firmly at one of His Lordship's legs, as if they meant to rend him apart.

His Lordship paled considerably. Next to infants, nothing could disconcert his composure more than small children. "Did you see the monster Boney in Vienna?" demanded Augustus, tugging at his father's coattails. "Does he have horns, like nurse says he does, and breathe fire?"

Lord and Lady Southcote's second set of twins had not quite reached their eleventh birthday. Except for the way in which they were dressed, it was almost impossible to tell them apart. Both of them were dark, like their father, with identical missing teeth and sets of freckles. Since Hester's hair had been cut during her illness, she resembled her brother even more, for Augustus's had been allowed to grow out slightly during his recuperation. Having spent the morning in the arduous study of multiplication, they were full of high spirits, and Lady Southcote was hard put to restrain

17

them from disarranging their father's clothing while they clung to him, pelting him with questions.

"Are there lots and lots of people in Vienna? Do they all wear funny outfits, like the picture in our geography book?"

"Did you bring me a rocking horse from Vienna, as you promised you would?"

"When I grow up, Papa, shall I be a soldier like Guy, or a dull dog like Clare? I want to be like Guy—"

"Hester! Augustus! Your manners!" A gaunt female of indeterminate age appeared in the doorway, frowning at her charges. Reluctantly, Hessie and Gussie removed themselves from their father's lapels and gathered by their dragon's skirts. "I'm sorry, Your Lordship, but sometimes they will misbehave. It's due to their having been so spoiled while they were ill, I think," she said severely, in a tone that did not bode well for the twins.

The earl smoothed his cravat down, swiftly gathering up his gloves and case from the table. "Quite understandable. I believe I was the same way at their age. I trust I find you well, Miss—uh—Ipstone?"

That female nodded grimly. "Quite well, my lord."

His Lordship nodded vaguely. "Well, I'm off. I sail with the tide, you know." With last-minute instructions as to the disposal of his presents, His Lordship took himself off with an almost unseeming haste, satisfied that his domestic duties had been done.

"Family life is all well and good, Marham," he confided to his secretary as the barouche wheeled down the drive, "but damme, there's only so much of it a man should be required to endure."

In the meantime, Lady Southcote was attempting to explain to her children and Miss Ipstone exactly what His Lordship's visit had entailed.

"We are expecting an addition to the family," she said mistily, looking about her.

Cynthia blushed. "Oh, Mama, not again!" she exclaimed.

Miss Ipstone frowned severely upon her former charge. "Cynthia, if you please! I do not think that is what Lady Southcote had in mind! You must learn to restrain your tongue!"

"Is Mama increasing?" Hessie piped up, wide-eyed. "Can I have a baby sister?"

Lady Southcote shook her head. "No, my loves. Nothing of that sort. Your papa has come to tell me that through the most dreadful mistake, the children of a very old friend of his, an American gentleman, were removed from a ship carrying them home to America and taken to Plymouth. Since Papa is off to Ghent to work on a treaty between America and England, we have decided that it would be better if the children were brought here until the war is over."

"Will the war be over soon?" Gussie asked suspiciously. "Are they wild Indians? Will they scalp us?"

Lady Southcote shook her head. "No, they are just two small, motherless children, caught in the ravages of war." With more vividness than it deserved, she described the Admiral Bowditch Inn, and if it sounded to her listeners as if the Clement children were languishing in a dungeon with bread and water, it was entirely her fault.

Cynthia and the twins, who had grown up amidst their father's exotic visitors, accepted the situation for

19

what it was. "There is no other course you could possibly take, Mama!" Cynthia said at one point. "We must make the Clement children welcome here."

"Do you think they will have scalps and feathers in their hair?" Gussie asked hopefully.

"They may have my place in the schoolroom," Hessie offered generously.

Only Miss Ipstone was not impressed. When she was alone with her employer, her thin jaw began to quiver and her hands tightened in her lap. "Dear Lady Southcote, I must beg you to consider the influence on the children! Americans! It is not at all what one would wish for a gentleman's household!" She lowered her voice. "One is never quite sure that they are civilized! Only consider that dreadful Frenchman, that émigré Lord Southcote had staying here—the maids were all threatening to quit! And that Turkish man with his wives—"

Lady Southcote, who could not share her employee's fear and dislike of strangers, merely sighed. "Miss Ipstone, these are *children*, very much like Hessie and Gussie, I dare say. I met Mr. Clement in Paris and his manners were all that could be desired. I am sure," she said with finality, "that his children would never betray ill breeding."

Miss Ipstone, realizing by the firmness in Her Ladyship's voice that further protest would be useless, glumly took herself off to the schoolroom to read her charges a very stern lesson on manners and deportment in the presence of their father.

Having, she believed, settled the matter with Miss Ipstone, Lady Southcote next called in her butler.

Gibney was much too well trained to betray any surprise over what His Lordship might do next, but he emerged from the interview somewhat pale and tight-lipped.

"Direct two of the maids to open up the rose chamber and the blue room," he instructed the footman, adding, "Lady Southcote is expecting two visitors—two American children." With that, he strode off to inform the housekeeper that he was not sure he knew what the world was coming to when a gentleman like Lord Southcote would harbor the enemy in his own house.

In a matter of an hour, the news had spread through the household. Speculation ran high over Lord South-cote's intentions in housing two American children in the midst of wartime. Since no one knew very much about Americans, except that their country was at war with Britain for the second time in a few decades, less tolerant people were heard to remark upon the dangers of harboring snakes within the bosom, and wondering what the earl would do next. But children were children, after all, and not as interesting as adults.

By the time the rose chamber and the blue room had been aired and dusted, almost everyone had forgotten about the incident. Two more little ones could not possibly disrupt the order of Southcote Place.

No coach arrived from Plymouth that day or the next. But on Wednesday a light rain began to fall in the morning, turning the roads to slushy mud, and Lady Southcote began to wonder if her husband had indeed managed to procure the release of the Clement children.

She was just sitting down to compose a letter to her sister-in-law, whose husband was in the Admiralty, when Gibney announced that a post chaise was coming up the drive.

"Oh, dear! Cynthia!" Lady Southcote exclaimed, pulling on her shawl and rushing toward the door.

Lady Southcote brushed back the startled footman to stand on the portico, watching anxiously, as the mud-splattered coach drew up to the door.

"Are they here, Mama?" Cynthia asked breathlessly, coming to stand behind her mother.

"Yes! At last!" Lady Southcote answered, her eyes searching anxiously as the postilion jumped down from his saddle and assisted the coachman in unstrapping several large trunks from the boot of the vehicle.

"The poor children," Lady Southcote murmured, clutching her daughter's hand as the footmen ran forward to assist the postilion.

The door of the chaise swung open and several bandboxes and bags were handed down to the now-sweating postilion. Lady Southcote and her daughter peered into the darkness of the carriage, straining for the sight of the Clement children.

One, two, three, and finally no less than fourteen bandboxes and not less than six trunks were handed out of the vehicle and stacked up in the hallway.

By this time, all the occupants of Southcote Place were either peering from the windows or gathered in the hallway, agog with curiosity about the new arrivals.

Gussie and Hessie joined their mother on the porch, having escaped the watchful eye of Miss Ipstone in order to witness the arrival, and their exclamations of awe and wonder were suddenly silenced as the postilion handed down two enormous brass cages containing two loudly protesting, brightly colored birds.

"Ooooh!" Hessie exclaimed, darting forward. "*Parrots!*"

Before Lady Southcote could protest, Gussie had joined his sister, and they were watching the birds from a safe distance with awed fascination.

"Blow me down!" one of the creatures shrieked, clinging angrily to the sides of its cage and fixing a baleful eye on the twins. The other bird, hearing his companion, immediately burst into a torrent of abuse in a language that none of the company understood.

Hessie was about to offer the smaller bird her finger when a voice said, "Please do not do that! They are very excited from the journey, you know, and apt to bite you severely. If you wait until they have settled down, they will behave themselves quite nicely, I assure you!"

A very tall young man had emerged from the coach, with a heavy volume under one arm of his plaid driving coat. A rather rakish beaver hat crowned his bright-red locks, and a pair of spectacles was perched on his nose. The smile he delivered to the assembled company was totally devoid of artifice. Rather absentmindedly, he closed his book against his finger and tipped his hat to Lady Southcote. "How do you do, ma'am?" he said in a slight, strange drawl. When his eyes rested on Cynthia, however, his pleasant face took on a look of total moonstrike, and a deep red flush crept up from the neck of his cravat across his high cheekbones. Slowly, he removed his hat once again, opening and closing his mouth. But no sound came out.

Fortunately, the company was diverted from these activities by the emergence of the second occupant of the post chaise.

First a glove of softest kid emerged and grasped the waiting hand of the footman, then one of the most dashing bonnets Lady Southcote had ever seen, supporting no less than three plumes, over a very delicate shade of Pomona-green velvet. Next, a foot shod in a neat kid half-boot appeared, and finally an altogether dashing velour pelisse of the same green as the bonnet, bound at hem and neck with jet frogs and tan braid. An ermine tippet was wrapped loosely about the hussar neck of the pelisse, and an enormous ermine muff was draped over one arm of the young woman who stood before Lady Southcote, holding out a hand to her startled hostess.

"How do you do, ma'am?" the young woman said, her voice deep and musical. Lady Southcote found herself gazing upward into a pair of enormous green eyes fringed with black lashes, while a broad good-natured mouth smiled at her. "I am Theodosia Clement. And you must be Lady Southcote. How kind of you to allow us to come to stay with you!" Her Ladyship found her hand being grasped very firmly by a very good tan grip, and it was several seconds before she could find her voice.

"But I thought you were—both of you—children!"

Theo Clement shook her roan curls. "Oh, no, ma'am! We haven't been children for ages!"

Scarlet with embarrassment, Jefferson Clement tore his gaze away from Cynthia's beauty and tipped his hat once again. "No, ma'am, we're not children. I'm eighteen and Theodosia is practically an ape-leader—she's *twenty!*"

"I—I see!" Lady Southcote murmured.

CHAPTER TWO

It said a great deal for Lady Southcote's manners that she was perfectly able to conceal a stunned dismay behind a polite smile. Far from being the two country waifs adrift in a strange land that she had allowed her kind heart to picture, the Clements seemed to be a pair well up on the world, sophisticated enough to make a cheerful front upon their present unfortunate situation.

Miss Clement cast her brother a quelling look, but laughter was not far from her eyes. "It's true, ma'am, I am, as you can see, long past the time I put up my hair and let down my skirts! And this rueful popinjay is my poor brother Thomas Jefferson Clement. You must not allow us to disrupt your household, for we agreed on our way up from Plymouth that we could do our absolute best not to provoke you, for you have been so very kind as to take us in!"

Lady Southcote murmured some polite phrases, but in the back of her mind she was experiencing the most unpleasant thought that these Americans were somehow under house arrest and she was to be their gaoler.

"Blow me down!" shrieked the smaller of the parrots, clinging to the sides of its cage and glaring at her in the most disconcertingly human fashion. "Blow me down!"

Gussie clapped his hands excitedly. "If you please, miss, may we feed the birds?"

Miss Clement's plumes nodded elegantly. "Of course you may, and I am certain that Jeff would be glad to show you how it must be done. But I fear they are a trifle cross with people they do not know well, you see. I daresay in time you may be able to teach them to speak properly. But I think, right now, they should be moved indoors. Parrots come from a tropical climate and do not take well to cold weather, you see."

The twins, interpreting her speech as an assent to their custody of the birds, each gave a loud whoop and bore the cages away into the house. Miss Ipstone, casting her eyes to heaven, and then toward the lesser light of Miss Clement, followed them with a sniff.

Lady Southcote felt constrained to protest, but Jefferson Clement intervened, with a charming smile. "I hope you don't mind, ma'am, but Theo and I had them as a gift when we were small, from the Bey, and—"

"Oh, Mama, please do let them stay," Cynthia said softly, "They are quite beautiful, and I am certain that they will afford the twins a valuable lesson in the science of biology and natural history—"

"You must be Lady Cynthia!" Theodosia Clement exclaimed. "I recognize you from your miniature. Your papa told me that you were as beautiful as your mama, but I declare, you surpass even the Doge's second wife, and she, you must know, is considered the Pearl of the Mediterranean!" Catching Cynthia's doubtful expression, Miss Clement broke off, laughing, and seized the girl's hand in her own. "Forgive my wretched tongue! I have been so long in Italy that I have adopted the manner of saying whatever comes into my head!"

Cynthia relaxed immediately, laughing and deciding that she liked Miss Clement very much.

"Frankness?" Jefferson laughed. "Her frankness has gotten her into more scrapes— When the Elector said—"

"I am certain that the Southcotes do not wish to hear about our experiences, Jefferson. Papa says nothing is more dull-witted than to drone on about one's adventures. Besides, it all worked out, did it not? Papa got his trade agreement and the Elector's sister married the proper man, after all, so it is unimportant." Miss Clement broke off laughing. "Oh, forgive me, ma'am. I think people who rattle on about their adventures are very dull dogs indeed, and I did not mean to bore you."

Lady Southcote, suddenly aware that her entire household was drinking in every detail of this scene, hastily suggested that her guests might like to move into the house. "You must be perfectly exhausted after your ordeal, quite dreadful," she murmured. "I can assure you that here, at least, you shall receive every consideration. Perhaps you would like to wash and have a rest, a mild repast of some sort . . . ."

"Ordeal?" Theodosia's voice was puzzled as her hostess slipped a hand into her arm. "I must say that we were—with *one* exception—treated with every consideration, ma'am."

"A repast sounds to be just the thing!" Jefferson said, allowing Cynthia to escort him through the portals. "I haven't eaten since lunch!"

"And I, dear ma'am, must say that I am glad we are

here! Only think how dreadful it would have been to be captured by Barbary pirates, and have to go to Tunis or Algiers, where one does not speak a word of the language, and would constantly be worried about saying 'Does your foot slip in the well?' when one means to say 'How are you today?' Indeed, it is bad enough to translate English into German, and then German into Italian . . ." Miss Clement shrugged. "Indeed, it is a very nice thing to be in a country where one speaks the language. . . ."

Lady Southcote, thinking of Fates Far Worse than Death which could befall young ladies in Arabic countries, shuddered.

"Oh, but I forgot!" Theodosia was saying, digging into a capacious pocket of her traveling pelisse to produce two tissue-wrapped parcels. "You will forgive the humbleness of these gifts for yourself and Lady Cynthia, but we were hardly prepared to be entertained in England—"

No woman can resist a gift, no matter how humbly wrapped, and when the tissue paper was removed to reveal two exquisitely wrought reticules of softest Milanese leather, hand-tooled in gold, both ladies were in raptures and put quite into charity with their two visitors.

Even Cynthia, in general so careless of her appearance, slipped the tiny bag over her arm, turning this way and that to admire the soft blue color of the leather, was forced to admit that Miss Clement must have second sight, for blue was exactly her color.

"My dear, I am certain that you meant these for some relation or friend in America," Lady Southcote said firmly, with only the twinge of regret in her voice

28

as she admired the mauve packet. "You must not feel that you must stand upon company manners and make them a present to us, my dear."

Jefferson shook his head lazily. "Oh, no, ma'am," he drawled. "Our only relation is an irascible grandmother, and she's a Quaker and don't hold with feminine fripperies."

"Oh, no," Theodosia said quickly. "Please, you must have them. I bought them only with the thought of someday bestowing them upon some unknown persons as gifts." She smiled. "And if I do not have second sight, I must pride myself upon choosing exactly the right colors for each of you!"

"Such charming manners," Lady Southcote murmured to her daughter as the Clements were shown to their chambers by the butler. "And such handsome people. Why, one would hardly know they were Americans."

Cynthia smiled. "Mama!" She said reprovingly, but she too was secretly pleased with their unexpected guests.

Jefferson, in his nightshirt, was lying across his bed, his glasses perched on the end of his nose, his candle guttering on the nightstand, as he turned the pages of the book on his stomach, frowning slightly at the opinions of William Pitt on government.

There were three soft knockings on the adjoining door between his room and his sister's, and at the familiar signal he rapped thrice on his headboard.

Theodosia, her hair let down for the night and her nightgown covered with a brocade robe embroidered with dragons, opened the door a tiny crack and peered all about. "Are there guards posted in the hallway?" she whispered, before padding across the floor in her bare feet and casting herself carelessly down on the foot of her brother's enormous bed. From the pocket of her robe she withdrew an apple and tossed it at Jefferson, who caught it in one hand and took a hungry bite.

"No guards," he said with his mouth full. "In fact, they seem like rather nice people to me. The kind of folks you'd meet anywhere."

Theodosia looked about her brother's room with interest. "This house looks like something from the Castle Garden Theatre's sets. Lord, Jeff, I wonder if Henry the Eighth slept in your bed. Lady S. tells me that some nasty princess or other once used my room. And it's so cold in there that I could believe she's still haunting the place." She shuddered slightly, pulling her robe closer about her shoulders. "One of the maids slipped me that apple. She was afraid that we hadn't had enough to eat."

"Enough to eat?" Jeff asked. "I got up from the table feeling as if I'd been stuffed as the Christmas goose. Theo, you have no idea what it was like to have to sit there with that butler glaring at me while I tried to drink one glass of port all alone. I *hate* port."

"I had a very nice time withdrawing with Cynthia and Lady S. Cynthia's talent at the pianoforte is quite above the usual missish drivel. She has a gift, that one. Oh, Jeff, I do like them. They're very nice people, and they're trying very hard to adjust to us."

"Cynthia's very nice. I like her a great deal," Jefferson said.

Theodosia gave her brother a strange look. "I noted

that you were most attentive to her, turning the pages while she played. I've never seen you pay any girl that much attention before."

Jeff shrugged. "I like her. She reads and doesn't carry on like a chicken, the way most young girls do." He frowned.

"Oh, Jeff—you mustn't start to like her too much—it will make things even more complex than they already are! Doubtless Lord Southcote will want to match her off to some other title, and some rustic hayseed from America will be a hindrance."

"I know," Jeff replied shortly. He bit at the apple. "Theo," he said at last, "what *are* we going to do? We're in the devil's pit for sure, as Old Burr would say."

Theodosia sat up, frowning into the fire. "I suppose we shall have to be on our best manners all the time. They've been nice enough to take us in—it was a choice between this and some prison hulk, remember, Jeff."

"I haven't forgotten," he said shortly. "But Theo, for all they may treat us like guests, my girl, we're still prisoners, and America *is* at war with England. We can't exactly expect people to welcome us with open arms, y'know?"

Theodosia nodded. "I know, as well as you do. We're swimming in water above our heads, no matter how well it looks on the surface. If only Father were here to advise us as to what to do!"

"He's not. Probably thinks we're safe in New York by now," Jeff said gloomily. "Which we're not. And if this war takes a turn for the worse, what's to become of us?"

"Devonshire Prison, I suppose," Theodosia replied matter-of-factly. "But I don't think either of us should like it very much. I've never been in prison, but I remember the one the elector kept beneath that castle—Rats, Jeff, and the smell—"

"No need to tell me, m'girl. I was there with you. And I doubt that we could expect much better. I don't worry about me so much as I worry about you, Theo."

She shook her head. "No, I worry about both of us. Jefferson, we shall simply have to behave ourselves, be very nice to the Southcotes, and stay out of trouble."

Jefferson took a bite out of the apple. "That's why I worry about you, Theo—you and trouble come hand in hand, sister!"

His sister threw him a speaking look, but only rose from the bed. "Well, I can't say that it's not pleasant to be lodged in this old pile—that's what they call these houses here—but Jeff, whatever we do, wherever we go, we will be watched. And they won't be judging us simply on our manners, brother dear."

With those final words, she closed the door.

Jefferson lay staring into the fire for long moments. But it was not in his nature to worry about the material world. With another large bite of apple, he returned to his book. Whatever happened, he knew that Theodosia would pull them about. She nearly always did.

Miss Clement and Lady Southcote both shared the custom of rising late and taking only a cup of chocolate in bed before starting the day, and the twins were safely breakfasted under the watchful eye of Miss Ipstone in the schoolroom.

Lady Cynthia had been so long in the habit of

breakfasting alone in the morning that she had acquired the habit of bringing her book to table with her and reading before she took her morning ride, as she drank her coffee and picked absently at her food. She was thus occupied when Jefferson Clement appeared hesitantly in the doorway, following the nearly incomprehensible directions of the West Country butler.

"Is this the breakfast room?" he asked shyly.

Cynthia was so startled that she dropped her book face down across the cloth. Seeing that it was the American house guest, she remembered to smile. "Yes. You must be seated, and I will ring for a fresh pot of coffee for you, Mr. Clement."

Jefferson awkwardly placed himself opposite her, placing his hand against the silver pot. "This seems warm enough," he murmured, pouring a cup.

"There are hot plates on the sideboard. Kidneys, eggs, muffins . . ." She suggested, a trifle flustered.

Jefferson shook his head. "No, I think I'll just have a cup of coffee at first, if you don't mind. It always takes me a while to get going in the morning."

They were both silent for several strained minutes while Jefferson poured cream and sugar into his cup and sipped at the brew. "I understood that most English preferred tea," he said at last.

Cynthia looked down at her plate. "Most do. But Papa introduced us to the custom of coffee, and I am rather partial to it in the morning, before I ride."

"Oh," Jefferson said. He glanced out the window. The day was overcast and gray, with the threat of rain. "Lovely day," he remarked.

She started. "Oh—yes, isn't it? I suppose you must

33

find our weather a bit drab. I understand that—that the sun shines quite a bit in America."

"Oh, it's sunny enough," Jefferson said.

There was a long silence, each one casting about for something else to say.

Jefferson took a deep breath. "If you'd like to go on with your book, it wouldn't offend me, Miss Southcote. I'm rather fond of reading at table myself."

Cynthia allowed the faintest hint of a smile to escape her lips. "Do—I mean, are you? I know it is deplorable manners, but when one is generally alone in the mornings, it—"

"It can be quite the nicest time of day to read," Jefferson finished for her. "What is the book?"

She turned her fingers down on the spine of the book. "Oh, just a novel . . . you must think me very silly to be reading novels."

Jefferson shook his head. "Not at all. One of the greatest books in Western civilization, *The Prince*, is written in the form of a novel. Machiavelli, you know."

This elicited a laugh from his companion. "I'm afraid that this is not quite *The Prince*, but it is very droll, and ever so much better than most of the fiction I have read. It's called *Emma*, and it's written by 'A Lady,' and it is all about the way people really are—no burning castles and falling helmets and all that sort of thing. I like it very much."

"About real people? I'd like to read it when you're finished—if I may," Jefferson said shyly.

"Of course," Cynthia replied.

There was a stretch of silence, during which the second footmen entered the room and inquired if the young gentleman would care for something not available at the sideboard. "For Mr. Gibney says that Americans may not be used to our foods," he finished, looking at Jefferson curiously.

Jefferson assured him that eggs and kidney were quite all right, and the young footman withdrew to tell belowstairs that the Yankee was conversing bookish with Miss Cynthia.

"We have a good library here at the Place," Cynthia ventured. "I beg you to make free of the volumes, since you like to read as much as I do. No one else uses it very much except Clare—but he is so rarely here except to come down with a heavy hand upon us all that I doubt very much if he would mind, that is—" Cynthia broke off, blushing.

"Clare?" Jefferson asked.

"Oh, Claremont, my brother. He's in the F.O. Since Papa is often abroad, or otherwise preoccupied with his work, Clare and Guy have been wont to keep an eye on the family—they were twins, you know," Cynthia continued artlessly. "Except, since Guy was killed in Spain, Clare has been impossible. He runs us all as if we were some sort of extension of the F.O. Oh, I do miss Guy—he was the happy twin, always coaxing Clare out of his sullens, or making him unbend just a trifle. But Mama says twins have a *bond*, and that Clare will probably never recover from the wound of losing his *other half*. But Clare can be so disapproving of the slightest mischief, and I fear that he is having a sad effect upon us all. Oh! I talk much, much too much, Mr. Clement! You must forgive me for rattling on like this!"

Jefferson shook his head. "Not at all, Lady Cynthia. All my life I've been under Theo's eye—she's two years older than I am, and inclined to be bossy, always going on about how I shall ruin my eyes with reading, to sit up and make conversation with dead bores at banquets—oh, you know. But I do love her, for all of that. Our mother died when we were both very young, and Theo's had a time of it, I guess, keeping Father and myself out of the trees."

"Oh, I did not mean to breathe a hint that I do not love Clare. It is just that older siblings can be so—"

"Oppressive, I think that's the word you want."

Cynthia smiled. "Exactly so. When one would prefer to be reading quietly, or having a ride, or doing—doing one's work, they are always there to remind one that dinner is being served and guests waiting, or that one must have one country dance with one's godfather's nephew who has spots and the most dreadful manners—"

They smiled at one another in perfect understanding. "That's right!" Jefferson said. "I'd much rather be left to my own devices than called upon constantly to perform like a trained monkey. And I'd imagine, for a girl, it's not much more tolerable!"

"Oh, to be female, Mr. Clement, is a sad state. Are you familiar with the writings of Mary Wollstonecraft? No? Then I fear you shall think me a sad bluestocking when I tell you that I agree completely with her view that woman should be entitled to all the rights and privileges of man!"

Jefferson frowned. "Theo says exactly the same thing, but never in public. And honestly, Lady Cynthia, I'm half inclined to support her position, now that I've met you. It's a pretty rare thing to meet an educated female—and frankly, I like it!"

Lady Cynthia Southcote smiled shyly. "I see," she said, toying with her napkin. "Perhaps—that is—would you like to see our library? It was catalogued several years ago, but since then, Clare has put in more volumes— We have some particularly fine translations of Horace that might interest you, as well as Pliny's entire *Natural History*."

"Very much!" Jefferson replied. "Lead the way!"

The barriers erected by a natural shyness on both their parts were agreeably eased by a half hour's browse through Lord Southcote's numerous volumes, and Jefferson began to have the feeling that his captivity would be eased considerably by the literature at his fingertips, as well as a companion to discuss his reading with. Theo was not bookish, and his tutors had been dry men of fact and a singular lack of imagination. To his delight and surprise, Lady Cynthia's mind was as quick and intelligent as his own; and this, combined with her singular beauty, was such a novel experience that he found himself conversing with her in the easiest manner possible.

For her part, Lady Cynthia Southcote had long been confined to the structures of her own imagination. Too well read and better educated than most females of her rank and station in life, it was a pleasure for her to discover in this tall blonde American a wit and intellect that matched her own.

Over Shakespeare they established themselves on first-name terms, the better to pour out their feelings about Hamlet and Cassius to one another. Over Richardson, whom they both disliked, and Fielding, for whom they both shared an interest, Lady Cynthia

Southcote felt impelled to confide to her new friend the darkest secret of her life.

"I am, you see, Jefferson, working on a novel!" she whispered.

"Are you, by God?" He grinned.

Cynthia turned away from the volumes lining the shelves, so that the light from the window fell about her shoulders in an aura of silvery beams. Whether it was the fairness of her hair or the pale tones of her ivory and buff riding habit it would have been hard to say, but Jefferson had the impression that this was no ordinary bit of female whimsy. "Yes. I know that it is most improper for a female to even dream of setting pen to paper to *write,* but I felt compelled to set down my imaginings upon paper. You must not tell any-one—Mama and Clare would both be very upset with me. But it is almost finished, and when I have completed it, I intend to send it off to a publisher in London!"

She lifted her chin defiantly. "Although no one knows about it but you, Jefferson, I know that I may trust you to keep your own council about my project. Mama would say that if it were put abroad that I wrote, it would quite spoil my chances of contracting an eligible alliance, and I should die an old maid!"

Jefferson wanted to smile, but did not. "Oh, I don't think so! Myself, I'd be proud as hops if I knew a girl who had published a book."

"You would?" Cynthia asked incredulously.

"Absolutely," Jefferson said firmly. "I'd feel very proud of any friend of mine who could have the discipline to sit down and complete an entire book! Cynthia—that is, well, if you'd like someone to look over your manuscript, maybe get a male opinion, even if it's just an American's—well, I'd be honored."

Her smile was almost devastating. "Oh, Jefferson! It would be so very nice to be able to *share* it with someone. I have tried, you see, to write like the author of *Emma*, and capture real people in real situations and—oh, but I shall let you look at it! I keep it hidden in the lower shelf of the library desk—no one else comes in here but me, so I have been able to write undisturbed and—oh! Miss Clement!"

Theodosia Clement, looking very refreshed for her night's sleep, entered the room, dressed in a forest-green habit of broadcloth, ornamented at neck and bodice with gold military braid. A long ochre plume swept past one ear of her shako cap, and in one hand she held a pair of neat buff gloves. It had often been said that Theo was at her best in riding attire.

"Good morning, Lady Cynthia; Jeff, dearest brother!" she exclaimed. "Miss Clement, your mother informs me that you ride in the mornings, and that you will be so kind as to allow me to accompany you! If it is at all inconvenient, please tell me so, for I have no wish to discombobulate you in any fashion!"

"Discom—discom—?" Cynthia repeated blankly, while she and Jefferson fell away from one another in confusion.

Jefferson gave his sister a quelling look that was returned with an even gaze. "It's an American word. It means to disorient or confuse," he said.

Cynthia nodded. "Oh, I see. Do you also care for riding, Jefferson? For we must take a tour of the stables and see how you can be mounted. I have a rather tame old plug, myself, Daisy, just for hacking about. I'm afraid I'm not a neck-or-nothing rider, but there are better mounts—"

Jefferson shrugged. "I am fond of riding, but not obsessed, like Theo. Lead on, Cynthia. We can continue our literary talk later, if you like. I did not know that I was keeping you from your riding!"

"Not at all! If you will come with me, Miss Clement, Jefferson," she said, leading them out of the room, "I think we can all be suited."

Theo, watching them leave, had the grace to allow two pink spots to appear in her cheeks. She loved her brother and felt a fondness for Cynthia's grave air and gentle manner. But that Jefferson should choose to experience his first love under these circumstances could be dangerous indeed for both of them. Unless, of course, she would be able to contrive. Theo's lips rose slightly. She was patient.

It was but the matter of a few good questions and a shrewd knowledge of horseflesh for Theo to reduce the suspicions of the elderly head groom to a sort of grudging respect for this tall American female with her strange accent and open manners. Leaving Cynthia to choose a suitable mount for Jefferson, Miss Clement accompanied Sexton through a thorough tour of Southcote Place's stables.

"Ar, it were nothing like, miss, when Mr. Guy was alive! He was a proper judge of horse! Mr. Clare, he's got good hands, and he knows his stuff, pardon me, miss, but Mr. Guy, he was, like, able to sense out a horse's character the way some men can judge one another down at the Pelican and Hart." The elderly man hooked his thumbs into his leather vest as they paused before the stall of a high-bred black gelding. The horse nickered and rolled its eyes, flattening its ears at the approach of humans. "This 'ere be Blood-and-Thunder, pardon the name, miss, bein' as how we calls 'im Thunder, my lady not likin' the sound of Blood. 'E was Mr. Guy's, and not another soul could ride 'im. Ar, to see them two crossing the fields and stiles like one creature, miss, it were something. 'E'll barely tolerate Mr. Clare on 'is back, and me to look arter, but it's Mr. Guy 'e misses, just as if 'e knew that 'e were slain on the battlefields." The old man shook his grizzled head. "Careful, now, miss, for 'e don't take kindly to strangers, bein' high-nervy in his way."

"Poor Thunder," Theo murmured. "How sad it must be for him, no one understanding his plight." Slowly, she extended her hand, palm outward, toward the giant black animal. It backed off a few paces, regarding her suspiciously, but she stood her ground, meeting its eyes. *"Hssssst, hssst,"* Theo murmured, keeping her hand steady.

Very slowly, she took one step toward the stall. *"Hsst, hsst,"* she repeated in the same low crooning tone.

"Careful, miss, Thunder's known to kick out his boards," Sexton warned, but Theo ignored him, concentrating on the horse, murmuring what seemed to be a great deal of nonsense beneath her breath, her hand inching slowly and steadily towards the beast's muzzle.

Reluctantly at first, the animal edged toward her hand, sniffing at her fingers. Still murmuring soothingly, she stroked the white blaze on the horse's nose with a feather touch. Slowly his ears inclined forward, and he pressed forward, sniffing, then nuzzling at her cheek. She reached up and scratched gently behind the horse's ears, and was rewarded with a sloppy lick of his long pink tongue against her cheek.

"Wal, I ne'er," Sexton said, scratching his head. "Miss, that hoss come arter you like you was his dam."

Theo continued to stroke the huge animal's head. "I think perhaps we understand one another. Often a bit of gentleness will work wonders where the whip can fail, you know. Do you think that he can be saddled for me?"

Cynthia, who had been watching Theodosia's performance with something akin to awe, exchanged a look with Sexton.

"Wal, miss, I ain't sure that Master Clare would like it, but it do need to be exercised—but he ain't a proper lady's mount, not by half!"

"Oh, Theo's got a way with horses. She can take on anything on four legs. M'father says she's got Gypsy in her when it comes to horses."

"But Miss Clement, if anything should happen to you—" Cynthia said doubtfully. "Oh, Clare would be so furious."

But Sexton had taken the measure of his rider and found nothing wanting, "Let us saddle 'im, then. 'E's got to have exercise, and it look that miss 'ere can handle 'erself."

"She's a bruisin' rider. If you'd seen her in the Piedmonts, in all weathers, you'd know that Theo's a complete hand!" Jefferson remarked, totally unconcerned.

In a very short time, Thunder was saddled and Miss Clement thrown up on his back. Thunder reared once or twice, feeling his freedom, but soon Miss Clement and the black gelding were dashing out of the stableyard and across the park at a most unladylike clip.

Sexton folded his arms across his chest and nodded. "Miss can do. And miss can do what's got to be done. Don't know what she's got, but it do work with that horse, almost as well as with Master Guy upon 'im," he remarked, watching closely as she brought the animal around the park and back up toward the stables. "Pluck to the backbone!"

There was a rumble of wheels, and they turned to watch a smart curricle tooling at a genteel pace up the drive, driven by a woman in a puce habit, with a liveried groom sitting behind.

Cynthia's face fell. "Miss Morton-West. Edwina. Oh, wouldn't you know that she would come along just at the wrong time?"

"Miss Morton-West?" Jefferson asked.

"She is Clare's fiancée," Cynthia said regretfully. "She's the daughter of Sir Henry, our neighbor. And she is Clare's spy upon us all!" She put a hand to her fair hair. "Oh, forgive me, I am uncharitable and boorish!"

The curricle pulled into the stableyard just as Theodosia completed her ride.

"Bruisin', miss! Bruisin'!" Sexton exclaimed admiringly as he handed Miss Clement down from her mount. "Ain't seen the like since Mr. Guy's day!"

Theo gave him one of her best smiles. "Thank you, Sexton! But I feel that it is the quality of Thunder rather than any mean abilities of my own that make him an excellent mount!"

With the aid of her groom, Miss Morton-West descended from the curricle and proceeded with a stately tread across the cobblestones, raising her parasol against the faint rays of the sun as she approached the group.

"Hullo, Edwina," Cynthia said without much life.

Miss Morton-West gave her future sister-in-law a thin smile. "Good day, Cynthia," she said in a tight, precise voice, her eyes ranging curiously over Jefferson. As she saw Sexton swinging Theo down from Thunder's back, her brows rose—but only slightly, for (she hoped) she was well bred enough not to betray surprise at the sight of a strange female in an entirely too dashing habit dismounting from a horse that was not only entirely unsuited to a lady, but also forbidden to anyone but her fiancé. When Theo slapped the dust from her broadcloth skirts with a mannish gesture and spoke frankly to Sexton about the stud condition of the horse, Miss Morton-West's long thin face took on a cast of definite disapproval.

"Oh—Edwina—Miss Morton-West, may I present Mr. Jefferson Clement? Mr. Clement and his sister are staying with us for a while," Cynthia said cautiously.

"How do you do, ma'am?" Jefferson said in his broad American accent, taking the limp hand that was presented to him with a sense of foreboding.

Everything about Miss Morton-West was thin. Her figure was long and lean, her face high-boned and narrow, her lips pressed firmly against one another, and her cool ice-blue eyes narrow beneath thin dark brows. Although she had been brought up to believe that vanity was a besetting sin of far too many females of her consequence and station, she was, however, well aware of the current fashion for thin and ethereal females, and had done her best to accentuate her own emacia-

44

tion with a driving dress of palest puce, adorned with the severest of ruffles, and a matching bonnet ornamented by a single riband of purple silk. Not so much as one curl escaped from the severe bands of her dark hair, and if there had been so much as one dangling thread about her person, she would have been cast into severe mortification.

Casting a critical eye over Cynthia, she noted that the girl's curls were running riot and that there was a stain upon the hem of her old and comfortable habit. Almost automatically, her gloved hand reached out to tuck an errant lock back into place, and Cynthia winced visibly.

"I have heard of your condition at Southcote Place. A most unusual situation, of course, but I felt, as Claremont's chosen, it was my duty to come over and offer what comfort I could, my dear. Really, you must learn, Cynthia, that it is not at all the thing to go about in that ancient habit with company present. And this must be . . ."

Theodosia was approaching the group, carelessly drawing off her gloves as her long stride brought her into their company. She hitched her skirts over one arm, and in a second had taken the full measure of Miss Morton-West with her shrewd eyes. The faintest smile played about her lips, and Jefferson knew then that his sense of foreboding was entirely correct.

"Uh—Miss Morton-West, Miss Clement," Cynthia stammered.

Edwina paused for the fraction of a second before extending her cold fingers to Theodosia, who gripped them firmly in her handclasp.

"Miss Clement is staying with us for a time."

"How do you do?" Theodosia murmured.

Miss Morton-West's smile grew a trifle more frosty. "Forgive me, Miss Clement, but I have been apprised of the awkwardness of your situation. As Lord Claremont Southcote's fiancé, I felt it to be my duty to drive over and offer what small assistance I may be capable of in helping you to adjust to what must certainly be an unpleasant situation."

Theo's face took on a look of puzzlement. "Unpleasant? Quite the contrary, Miss Morton-West, I have found the Southcotes to be the most considerate of hosts in what must certainly be an unusual situation for us all, but not entirely uncommon among those in the diplomatic service."

Miss Morton-West's lips parted slightly.

"You see," continued Theodosia calmly, "brought up, as both the Southcotes and the Clements have been, in a rather international way, we have learned early to contrive as best we may, one individual to another. It is my understanding that Lord Claremont Southcote is with your Foreign Office. Doubtless, as his bride, you will also soon contrive to adjust to strange people and situations."

Miss Morton-West uttered an inaudible gasp.

Jefferson Clement, who knew his sister very well, gently took Cynthia's arm, and with some remark about wishing to inspect the fine view of the hills from the aspect of the terrace, led her away.

Miss Morton-West recovered herself swiftly. "Of course, I am not completely without exposure of foreign influences, Miss Clement, but I must question—as Claremont's fiancé, of course, and his deputy *in absentia*—the propriety of riding a horse he has forbid-

46

den to anyone but himself. Such manners cannot, even in America, be considered well bred."

The slightest tinge of rose appeared in Miss Clement's cheeks, but she laughed. "No, and I am sadly at fault and shall have to tender my apologies to Mr. Southcote when we meet. But, as Sexton has pointed out, the animal is sadly in need of exercise, and one turn about the park can hardly be construed as damaging to either Thunder or Lord Claremont." She shook her head. "Miss Morton-West, I admit I have sinned dreadfully in this matter, and that I must bow to your superior judgment."

Edwina relaxed slightly. "I am so glad that you are willing to allow me to guide you in this matter, Miss Clement. What may be acceptable in America may not always be the correct thing in England. Here, after all, we try to maintain certain standards of conduct that must laxen a bit in the wildernesses of your country." Somewhat mollified, she inclined her head. "But I do not feel that this discussion should be conducted in a stableyard."

Theo glanced toward the curricle. "That is a very pretty set of equipment, Miss Morton-West. And I must say that I approve of your grays, although the left might be considered just a trifle high in the chest—in America, of course. Here, I know that you do things differently, and you must tell me how I am to go along." This remark was accompanied by such an innocent smile that Edwina was able to put it down to Miss Clement's inexperience in the proper world.

"I am considered a creditable hand," Edwina admitted. "Perhaps you would care to take a turn about the paths in the home wood with me, where we may con-

47

tinue our discussion with more privacy?" She threw a quelling look at Sexton, who suddenly found he had more pressing business in the tack room.

"Oh, I would be honored if you were to take me up," Theo said. "And of course, tell me how I might best conduct myself."

Although charity was not one of Miss Morton-West's virtues, she did feel a slight softening toward Miss Clement. Ever ready to impart the wisdom of her own experience and fine sense of propriety to others, she led Miss Clement toward the vehicle.

As they spun through the wooded paths, Edwina slackened the reins a bit and turned to Theodosia. "You must, of course, forgive me my bluntness, Miss Clement, but as Lord Claremont's deputy, I feel it is my duty to look after the Southcotes. Lady Southcote tends to be far too indulgent a mother, and both Cynthia and the twins frequently display a deplorable mischievousness that exceeds what Lord Claremont and myself consider to be the outside limits of propriety. Of course, Lord Southcote has his duties to the country, or I am certain that he would instantly put a stop to that most unbecoming lack of dignity the children so frequently display."

"I wonder," Theodosia replied flatly. "Lord Southcote himself is an arch-cynic, you know, and enjoys a very fine sense of liveliness."

"Miss Clement! You are speaking of one of England's most valued statesmen!"

"I speak also, Miss Morton-West, of a man who has been my father's dearest friend for many years and my brother's godfather," Theo said quietly. "Indeed, my brother and I have come to times when we depended upon his judgment as we would upon our own father's. There were certain difficulties for two young children confined to the etiquette of the elector's court that were resolved through his good advice—"

"The elector's court?" Miss Morton-West asked politely.

"It is of no consequence. I very much dislike people who prose on about their experiences. But you were about to tell me how I must conduct myself."

Miss Morton-West straightened her spine. "Let us speak frankly, then, Miss Clement. America and England are at war, and your brother and yourself are enemies of England and prisoners within her boundaried shores. It is of course an awkward situation for you, and I must say that I sympathize with your discomfort. But you are in a household of the highest *ton,* and it is necessary that you do nothing to inconvience of dismay your hostess."

"I am aware of that," Theodosia replied evenly, admiring the verdant woods through which they traveled.

"Of course, you cannot expect to go into society, even in the more limited company of the country. So, if Lady Southcote is invited out, or entertains at home, you of course, should politely absent yourself from company."

"I see. And would you suggest that my brother and myself eat our meals on a tray in our rooms rather than sit at table with the family?"

Miss Morton-West frowned over this question. "Yes, perhaps so. In fact, if you were to confine yourself to one another's company as much as possible, that might be better for all concerned. In England, after all, we do have certain standards of—well, one's birth and station to maintain that I understand do not exist in America. It would not do for you to be too forward, or to put yourself too much in the way of seeking out members of the *ton*. It would be considered most forward of you."

"I see. And tell me, also, from your experience, what should I do if, by the veriest chance, I should happen to encounter a member of the *ton?* Purely by accident, of course."

"Why you should simply bow, with all proper humility, and pass on your way. Do not speak without being spoken to, and never, never do anything to call attention to yourself."

"Yes, of course."

"You are, quite frankly, Miss Clement, an attractive female, in your own way, of course, so perhaps it would be better if you adopted a less-dashing mode of dress. Such a habit as you wear now cannot but attract attention to yourself, and that, at all costs, you must avoid."

"Oh, but my dear Miss Morton-West, I have no other clothes but what I have purchased in Italy, and I fear they are all much in the Parisian mode."

"Then you must strive to dress with more docility. Since you have not been presented at court, you will not be called upon to—well, dress quite so fashionably. A bit more modesty in your dress would not be amiss."

"And you have, I assume, been presented at court?" Theo asked, her lashed lids lowered.

"Of course. I have been out for three seasons now. So, perhaps, I may be said to know a bit more of the world than you."

"Oh, I see. Then if being presented at court constitutes being *out* in your country, I suppose I have always been out. I've been presented at the White House in America, at the elector's court in Hesse, at the Doge's in Venice and the prince's in Milan, as well. I suppose one could count my bow before Napoleon as something. . . ."

Miss Morton-West flushed. "That is not at all the same thing."

"No, I doubt that it is. But please, tell me what else I must do to not incur some censure upon my poor head."

They were now upon a narrow country lane that crossed through the Southcote lands, and were suddenly surprised when a sharp turn exposed them to a gentleman on horseback coming the opposite way. "Well," Miss Morton-West began to say, but Theodosia was not attending to her at all.

"Can that be—it is not possible—but of course!" She waved her hand. "Steyland!"

The gentleman broke into a canter and approached the curricle, peering closely at its occupants. Suddenly his saturnine countenance broke into a wide smile, and he reined in.

"By all that's holy, Theo Clement! Peerless Theodosia! Let me feast upon your face for a second, my girl. Then you must tell me what in the devil you're doing in Devon, of all places?"

"The Marquess of Torville!" Edwina whispered in awe and shock and that handsome gentleman swept off his high-crowned beaver and made a low bow over Theo's hand, pressing his lips against her glove, to the slight disarrangement of his exquisitely tied cravat.

"Steyland, Steyland! Lord, I never expected to see

51

you! I thought you were still in Germany, driving all the *fraus* to distraction with those piercing eyes!" Theo was laughing, delighted at seeing her old friend.

The marquess, still clutching her hand in his own, bent from his mount to peer into her face. "By God, Theo, you grow more lovely every time I see you— What has it been—four, five years since I led you through the steps of that infernal court dance? I thought you to be safe in New York by now—or, at the very least, the first wife of the sultan, for you were ever one for adventure! Peerless Theodosia! Wait until I scribble a note to Rumford an m'sister—and of course you'll want to see 'em all, won't you—Durning and Bakersfield, and young Fox—" The marquess straightened up in the saddle. Recalling his manners, he looked kindly upon Miss Morton-West.

"Oh, I shall have to explain everything to you in time, Steyland!" Theo laughed. "Although now that I know you're about, it doesn't seem to be *half* the tangle it was before. Jeff is here also, and we're under a sort of house arrest through the most ridiculous set of circumstances possible— Oh, Miss Morton-West, may I present Mr. Albert Steyland!"

"Not plain old Albert Steyland anymore, Theo! M'uncle stuck his spoon in the wall at last, and I'm now the Marquess of Torville!" He winked. "Devil's own title, ain't it? How do you do, Miss Morton-West? You must forgive me, but as you can see, it's been ages since last I saw the Clements. How goes your father? I trust he's not in this tangle also? By God, I must see Jeff—I'll wager he's shot up like a weed!"

"Oh, indeed he has. He's as tall as his namesake now, in his stocking feet. And Father is fine, as much as I know. In Ghent, seeking to put an end to this infernal war, with Lord Southcote. I imagine they spend a great deal of their time sampling the local wines, however—"

The marquess threw back his handsome head and laughed. "Yes! Exactly so! Ever the oenophiles, those two. Do you recall—no—I shall save our memories for later. I'd just come down from London to have a look-in at the old place, and I haven't been accepting invitations or extending them either—country's a dead bore, y'know? Shall you be coming to London, Theo? If you are, I'm certain my sister will do her best to get you vouchers for Almack's—it's this dance hall they've got running up there like an Arab marriage market— you'd have a laugh or two out of having a look-in at it—"

"Almack's Assembly Rooms can hardly be compared to an Arabian slave market, sir," Miss Morton-West put in, much shocked at the description of those august gatherings.

"Morton-West? Morton-West? Oh, of course, you must be Sir Henry's daughter, ma'am. I believe we are neighbors—yes!"

"Indeed, sir, my mother has extended you several invitations to rout parties and dances at our home. But you have always rejected us of the country society." Edwina's attempt at light banter was slightly false, and Theo found a genuine pity for one so lacking in humor.

The marquess frowned slightly. "Oh—what? yes, of course. Been busy, you know. Setting Torville Manor to rights has been a job of work, Miss Morton-West. But now that Theo's—I mean, now that I have things a bit more under control, I believe I shall have m'sister and Rumford down. London's sadly devoid of company, and I dare say, now that Debra's increasing, she'd be glad of some good Devon air and a chance to hostess for her old brother. Rumford's still as boat-mad as ever, Theo. He bought a yacht that you must sail upon! As yar as they come! But I shall throw the old pile open now that Theo's back, and have all the old company down to see you and Jeff! I dare say you're languishing from boredom, Theo. Of course, Lady Southcote's got a great heart; I dare say she'll be wanting to present you about the countryside, put you in with all the *ton!* By God, girl, you must come and take London by storm!"

"Oh, I doubt that I should cause a ripple of interest," Theo laughed. "But I should dearly love to see dear Debra and Harry and all of the lads—"

Since the persons of which Miss Clement spoke were all high members of the *ton,* Miss Morton-West could only stare.

The marquess nodded and smiled. "Won't we have a good time, though! Peerless Theodosia Clement! Tell me, is there any hope for me, or have you given your heart elsewhere by now?"

Theo laughed again. "Steyland, Steyland! Your manners!"

The marquess sighed and placed a hand over his heart. "It's always been you, Theo, and none other."

"If I believed that, Albert, I should be a bigger fool than I think I am. But you will come to call upon Lady Southcote, please?"

"Ah, Theo! Wild horses would not prevent me from calling upon you! But, I must warn you that I shall have to bring along my dull dog of a cousin, for he's been rusticated or whatever you may call it from the navy, and m'aunt's got it into her head that's my charge. Dull dog, no sense of humor at all. When we were boys, he was always runnin' to bear tales. But I dare say we shall contrive. Peerless Theodosia! If I were ten years younger, m'girl—" The marquess, who had all of thirty-one summers upon his handsome head, shrugged his elegant shoulders and rolled his eyes in a droll way that might have surprised his so-phisticated London acquaintances, who understood him as a cool hand and a Pink of the *ton*.

But Theo burst into laughter. "Albert, if you must shrug your shoulders, then you should at least give your tailor fair warning of the fashion! If you were twenty years older, my friend, I should still be con-cerned for my heart!" She gave his hand a gentle squeeze. "But you must know that you have had my heart since I was still dragging my dolls about with me, my friend."

The marquess flicked an invisible speck of lint from his immaculate riding coat and raised his famous dark brows mockingly. "Lord, Theo, never put it about that I fixed that accursed popper for you, or I shall com-pletely be sunk below reproach! Have a reputation as a cynic and a man about the town to maintain, y'know!"

"Your secret is safe with me, Albert," Theo promised merrily. "But we shall have time and more to speak of the old days soon enough. Please, do send for Debra, if she may still travel, for I yearn to see her and Rumford again. And it seems as if Jeff and I shall not be able to move about as much as we might like on this visit."

The smile still played about the marquess's lips, but

the glint of understanding in his eye was both sharp and sympathetic. "Count upon me, Theo! If you must be a captive, then we shall strive to make your captivity as pleasant as possible, my girl. Be that as it may, I cannot and will not keep you conversin' on the public highways with such a rogue as m'self! But count upon me to present m'self to Lady Southcote 'pon the morrow, and then we may have a comfortable coze and catch up on all the *on-dits!* If you find yourself sailing close to the wind—and knowin' you, you will, call upon me! Peerless Theodosia! Lord, what a dust-up this will cause in town! Servant, Theo, Miss—um—Morton-East."

With a flourish of his crop, the celebrated buck bid the ladies a good day. With one last promise to call upon the morrow at Southcote Place, he spurred his chestnut down the lane at an elegant pace.

During this conversation, the color had drained from Miss Morton-West's cheeks, and for all her piety upon good manners, she found herself hard pressed not to stare after the most ton-ish gentleman of Society, that elusive prize of the marriage mart who was upon such intimate terms with her American companion. When she recollected how her mama had sought in vain for the marquess's attendance at any social gathering these months past, only to be politely but firmly refused, then witnessed upon what terms her companion stood in his haughty esteem, she could not help but feel a distinct mortification and, more unpleasantly, a very definite sense of jealousy. Since Miss Morton-West had been brought up to believe jealousy was a besetting sin, she took elaborate pains to set up the pair again, trotting off at a brisk pace.

Theo lowered her lashes. Not so much as the tiniest smile escaped from her lips, and she folded her hands in her lap.

"As you were saying, Miss Morton-West?" Theo murmured demurely.

"The Marquess of Torville?" Lady Southcote's teacup rattled against her saucer and she looked from one to the other of her guests, trying yet again to conceal her surprise at the unexpected resources of the Clements.

Theodosia gently brushed a crumb of sugar from the skirts of her mint-green afternoon dress, frowning at Jefferson as he reached for his fourth tea-cake. From her experience with two strong sons, Lady Southcote knew that young men's stomachs are bottomless, and almost absently she passed a plate of éclairs toward Jefferson. "Yes ma'am. Do not be put out with me, please, for if it is not convenient to receive Steyland, perhaps we may be allowed to visit his home for an afternoon. I am certain that he would send a carriage for us and provide whatever you feel necessary in the way of proper chaperonage—" She sipped delicately at her tea, very much liking this English custom.

Lady Southcote shook her head. "Oh, no, my dear Theodosia! Of course he may call upon us! It is simply that any number of hostesses in the neighborhood have sent him a volume of invitations, and he has consistently refused them all. You must know that he is of the highest *ton,* and quite elusive. And—oh, I am rattling on! Of course, he must come! The Marquess of Torville—won't that set up that dreadful Honoria Morton-West's back when she finds that he will pay us a morning call? And I am certain that Edwina shall inform her."

"It will certainly put her nose out of joint," Cynthia put in mischievously. "Always droning on about her connections in the *ton*, and at the same breath, deploring fashionable society as frivolous!"

"Cynthia, my dear," Lady Southcote said, oblivious of her previous speech, "you must not say such things about Clare's future mother-in-law. The Morton-Wests are quite respectable," she added tonelessly.

Theo said nothing, even though she had listened to this exchange with acute interest.

Lady Southcote touched the ruffles of her cap, her face triumphant. "Lord Torville! Coming to call upon us! Well, he shall certainly be made welcome, dear Theodosia. For your sake as well as our own." A slight frown creased her brow. "I understand that he is a dreadfully high stickler, however. Shall he expect us to serve sherry or ratafia for a morning call?" She bit her lip. "Clare frowns upon entertaining in the country, and really, since Guy's death, we have done so little entertaining at all that I have quite forgotten my manners. . . ."

"Do not worry, ma'am," Theo said soothingly. "I think you will find that Steyland's reputation is much larger than life. I think perhaps it is more a sense of being afraid of boredom that keeps him away from the usual routines of Society—as I understand it. But I am certain that in your charming and comfortable household, you will find him a very easy person indeed."

"Oh, dear," Lady Southcote said. "Lord Torville—here!" She smiled. "Jefferson, do have another éclair. Theo, what shall I wear?"

CHAPTER THREE

"The best sherry, of course, Gibney!" Lady Southcote said, her hands darting for the hundredth time that morning to an exquisite arrangement of hothouse flowers that needed not one iota of attention. "And the tea tray—for, of course, we must have the tea tray!"

Gibney, who had been in service with Lord Southcote far too long not to know exactly what refreshments were required for a morning call in the country, merely nodded with considerable forebearance and strove, in his most professional manner, to assure Her ladyship that all details had been personally supervised by himself.

As usual, this seemed to have a calming effect upon Her Ladyship, for she bestowed a grateful smile upon her retainer and assured him that she indeed would never know how to go on without him, but did he not think that pink and white roses were a trifle *jejune* for a marquess?

"For a marquess, Milady, pink and white. An earl or a duke, perhaps red roses. But a marquess, pink and white would seem to be appropriate," Gibley said tonelessly, and took himself off belowstairs to inform the housekeeper that the Young American Person had managed to snare the Lion of the countryside, and he would give a groat to see that widgeon-faced butler of the Morton-West's when he heard the news.

At that moment, the Young American Person entered the drawing room, fetchingly attired in a morning dress of cornsilk muslin, ornamented with ribands of ivory silk embroidered with the smallest chains of green ivy. Her reddish-brown curls were charmingly dressed *à la Meduse,* and a pale green Pointe-de-Russie shawl was draped carelessly over her arms. Seeing her hostess's agitated flutterings, she was immediately struck with guilt.

"Oh, dear ma'am, please do not put yourself out on Steyland's account. Indeed, if Jefferson and I had thought that his call would cause you the least trouble, I am certain that we could have contrived an afternoon at Torville—" Theo began in genuine concern, but Lady Southcote placed a reassuring hand on her arm.

"Dearest Theodosia, I know not how you have contrived it, but you have snared the social prize of the neighborhood! Put me out? My child, every hostess in the county has tried and failed to lure Lord Torville into her household, and he has steadily refused us all? I assure you, Theo, that as little as I may care for the snares of the *ton,* even I cannot but feel a certain very un-Christian pride in being able to receive the marquess at Southcote Place!" She gave her fluttering smile. "It is very ungenerous of me to even say such a thing, but I feel that I may confide in you, Theodosia, that I shall thoroughly enjoy seeing Honoria Morton-West's nose put out of joint when she hears that Torville has come to call upon us!"

Theodosia sighed with relief. "I am so glad that you

do not feel put out! I certainly did not mean to overextend when Steyland promised to call—"

Lady Southcote shook her head. "Overextend? Theodosia, you have performed a miracle!"

Miss Clement frowned. "Well, I have always considered Steyland to be a bit interesting, ma'am, but I doubt that he is miraculous!"

But Her Ladyship only shook her head. "Dear child, you do not yet know the ways of Society in England. Any hostess worth her reputation would give her right arm to have Torville put in as much as five minutes at one of her parties!" She fondly shook her head at Theo's naïveté and smiled brightly. "But I dare say you shall contrive! Imagine standing upon such terms with Torville!"

Theodosia shrugged, then laughed. "They are but the terms of friendship of long standing, ma'am. In a foreign land, it is quite normal for people with the bonds of language and culture to be drawn to one another. Steyland was on his grand tour with his tutor, and my brother and I were with our father at the elector's court. It was only natural that we should all study German with the same strange little professor. . ."

Lady Southcote glanced at the clock. "Oh, where is Cynthia? I do hope she has changed into her morning dress. If she should receive in that dreadful habit, I shall perish from embarrassment."

"I believe she and my brother are in the library, ma'am. I chanced to hear them talking as I passed."

"Bookish! Entirely too bookish!" Lady Southcote sighed distractedly. "Theodosia, I do not mind confiding in you that it has been a sad cross for a mama to bear. Cynthia is almost wrenchingly lovely—even I, her mama, must admit that. But the moment she opens her mouth, such bluestocking phrases, such bookishness—well, it drives the men quite away! And I do believe she might have had the Duke of Coldstone if she had only not spoken about that dreadful Wollstonecraft female—" Lady Southcote sighed. "Dear Theo, there is something about you that makes one want to confide one's worries—it must be terribly tiresome for you to hear me prattle on so, but I do worry about her—why, she is seventeen, and no offers! Another season, and she shall be quite upon the shelf!"

Theo inclined her head slightly. "I am twenty, ma'am, practically what you might call an ape-leader, and I am not at all bookish. But I feel that Cynthia will contrive a good match, for surely there is a man out there who appreciates both brains and beauty in a girl!"

Lady Southcote looked doubtful, but Theo's words had such conviction behind them that she was almost able to feel a glimmer of hope. She studied the young woman before her closely, and once again had the uncomfortable feeling that Miss Clement had far more resources at her fingertips than one might suppose from her American background. After all, the Marquess of Torville . . .

"Do you sit down and make yourself comfortable, ma'am. I shall go and make certain that my brother and Cynthia are both ready to receive morning callers." As she spoke, Theo arranged the cushions on Lady Southcote's favorite chair, fetched her Norwich shawl and her work basket, and left Her Ladyship a bit more calm.

But really, if one just moved that single white rose-bud a trifle to the left . . .

" '. . . upon which, Mr. Fairmount raised his brows slightly, and put a hand against his lips. If Miss Elizabeth was conscious of the slightest trace of a smile playing across his features, she gave no notice, but turned her attention gravely upon Lady Caroline.' "

Just outside the library door, Theo paused for a second to disentangle the fringes of her shawl. Cynthia's reading voice continued. " '*I*, of course, must feel that such manners are to be expected in a vicar! After all, where else should we procure Christian charity?" Lady Elizabeth said archly.' "

Jefferson's laughter burst through the room. "That's good—that's very good! Lady Caroline is a perfect fool, Cynthia!"

"Oh, then you do see her, Jefferson. I am so very glad. I was afraid that when I created her, she might be too broad or too subtle—"

"No, not at all! She's a card, for sure!" Jefferson's voice replied. "Cynthia, you've got, well, you've got talent, and no mistake! If I were a smart publisher, I'd snatch that up—"

Theo frowned and took a deep breath. Feeling like an ogre, she rapped her knuckles gently on the door frame and stepped into the room.

Immediately, two blonde heads parted, and a bit of paper was thrust into a drawer. Two pairs of guilty eyes met her steady gaze, and Miss Clement was conscious of the most unpleasant sensation of being cast into the role of a villain.

Although there were those who might say that Theodosia Clement had more than her share of nerve, it wrenched her to be forced to drive a wedge between two young people so obviously suited to one another. But she smiled as she came into the room, apologetically shaking her head. "I'm sorry to intrude, but Lady Southcote wished me to ascertain that you were both ready to receive Steyland—Lord Torville."

Jefferson scowled at his sister, and Cynthia's delicate complexion was suffused with a rosy blush as she stood up and shook out the skirts of her white muslin dress. "Yes, of course," she murmured. "You are quite right—we all should be in the drawing room. . . ."

As Jefferson passed his sister, he gave her arm a very hard pinch, an action he had not resorted to since childhood. Worried, Theo caught his arm, seeking to convey by looks and gestures that it was not up to her, but that—Jefferson only pushed his glasses up on his nose, thrust his hands into his pockets, and trailed Cynthia out of the library, leaving his sister with a worried expression on her face.

"What would Father do?" she mused aloud. "If it were only under any other circumstances than *these* . . ."

She decided that she must contrive to have a private word with Steyland. Albert, after all, was almost as good as Thaddeus Clement.

Lord, what a tangle! she thought, picking up her skirts and trying to proceed with as much dignity as possible toward the drawing room.

She was not pleased to enter the room just as Edwina Morton-West was being relieved of her bonnet and pelisse by Gibney, nor, as Theodosia's quick eye took in, was Lady Southcote, who was doing her best to conceal her annoyance at this unexpected call beneath a mask of politeness.

"Ah, good day, Miss Clement," Edwina said coolly, surveying the American lady's gown with a look that made it entirely clear that she considered such French finery entirely too sophisticated. "I was just telling dear Lady Southcote that being in the neighborhood to inform the vicar that one of his flock had transgressed the Seventh Commandment with the blacksmith's daughter, I thought I might make the liberty of a call. I always write to Clare—Mr. Southcote—upon Thursdays, and I particularly wished to see if there was any information I might convey to him in the post." With a smooth gesture, she spread the skirts of her mauve dress beneath her on the chair, folding her hands primly in her lap.

"Quite so," Lady Southcote said tonelessly.

"If you mean, Edwina, that Jemmy Raske has been walking out with little Mary Keene, I doubt very much that they've been violating any commandments," Cynthia put in gently. "Their banns have been posted for two weeks, and with both of them coming from such large families, it would hardly be a wonder if they sought walks in the country to be alone together without small brothers and sisters tagging about."

Edwina's back stiffened slightly, but she delivered a thin smile toward Cynthia that made the girl cringe. "We of the upper orders must always be prepared to guide our inferiors upon matters of moral conduct. And so I informed the vicar. After all, such matters are his duty." Her smile showed an even row of small white teeth. "Unfortunately, Reverend Woodall is quite unworldly. I sometimes think that when Clare—that is, when I am Lady Southcote—I shall have to see about replacing him with someone a bit more equipped to guide the flock of the parish."

"Indeed," Lady Southcote said, and her tone was not pleasant. She might have said more if Gibney had not chosen to announce Lord Torville and Lieutenant Steyland at that moment.

"Lieutenant Stey—" Jefferson exclaimed, but Theo put a restraining hand upon his arm.

Torville, resplendent in a buttermilk coat of superfine and a pair of very well fitting pantaloons, strolled into the room. There was, Theo had to admit to herself, a very definite gleam of mischief in his eyes, and when she recognized the slight, stoop-shouldered figure in naval uniform following upon his footsteps, she immediately understood why.

"Lady Southcote, may I present Lord Torville?" Theo said a trifle breathlessly, "Miss Southcote, Lord Torville—you remember of course Miss Morton-West—and Jefferson, of course you know—"

Torville bent gallantly over Lady Southcote's hand. "Madam, I am honored. I have heard much about Southcote Place, and about your prowess as a horticulturist. . . . Miss Southcote, Miss Morton-West, servant, ladies. May I in turn present, to those of you who have not yet had the honor, my cousin, Lieutenant Peter Steyland?"

The lank young officer, who had been looking from one Clement to another with an expression that could only be described as horrified recognition, recovered himself with some effort to make stiff bows in the direction of the other ladies.

"I believe my cousin already has made acquaintance

with Miss and Mr. Clement," Torville murmured wickedly. "I thought it might be interesting to renew the acquaintance." Having thus delivered himself of a most impish grin in Theo's direction, he proceeded to charm Lady Southcote and the other two ladies with all of his considerable powers.

"Lieutenant Steyland," Theodosia said quietly, holding out her hand. "Albert's little jokes are not always as humorous as he would like to find them, I fear."

Jefferson merely crossed his arms across his chest, glaring at the other man from beneath his spectacles.

Lieutenant Steyland hesitated for one infinitesimal second before allowing his long, cool fingers to brush against Miss Clement's hand. "Indeed, Miss Clement," he said coolly. "In fact, I have always found his sense of humor to border on the extreme edge of bad taste." The corners of his thin mouth drooped. "It is not pleasant, ma'am, to be confronted with the very cause of one's disgrace."

Theo reddened slightly, but kept her composure. "Since we are no longer your prisoners, Lieutenant Steyland, perhaps we may contrive to cry civility, if not friendship. Indeed, I am very sorry that we are, if Albert is correct, the cause of your present absence from your career."

"My career, madam, is my life. And I deem it necessary to inform you that because of you, I have received what I can only describe as a monumental setback!"

"Well, you have no one to blame but yourself, then!" Jefferson hissed angrily, his fists clenched. "We carried papers of neutrality, and by the laws of international diplomacy, you were bound to recognize them, instead of seizing our ship! Because of you, eleven men are languishing in one of those floating hells you people choose to call prison ships, and my sister and myself find ourselves safe only through the kindness of friends!"

Lieutenant Steyland's long face tightened and he looked down his nose at the angry young man before him. "In times of war, there are rules, Clement! Rules that must be followed! If your blasted little wilderness of a country hadn't chosen to bite England in the backside at the very time that we were fighting for our lives against Bonaparte—"

"Gentlemen!" Theodosia whispered. "Keep your voices down! We are all guests in another's household, and there are ladies present! I, for one, am willing to call quits. We three were all placed in a most unfortunate situation, but it is over now, and I believe that we are all civilized people." Again she held out her hand. "Please, let us say no more upon it. Even now, our two countries strive to make peace—"

Steyland clasped his hands behind his back and bowed stiffly. "I am a man of war, Miss Clement. I recognize no quarter, nor do I give any! And from what I have seen of you, believe me, I shall keep a sharp eye upon your doings in this neighborhood, for you are not to be trusted!"

With this harsh speech, the man turned his back on the Clements.

Theo's hand sought Jefferson's, and she squeezed hard. Fortunately, Lady Southcote had not witnessed the ugly scene that had just passed, for Torville was practicing his much-vaunted charm to good effect.

But the sharp eyes of Edwina Morton-West missed nothing, and she sighed sympathetically for poor Lieutenant Steyland, who, after all, had only been doing his duty. Really, she thought, running her black mitts through her fingers, Miss Clement far exceeded herself; the poor American female was much too forward.

Lord Torville swiftly showed himself to be an amiable person, easily entertained and unwilling to stand too long upon ceremony. When it was discovered over sherry and biscuits that he was very much interested in erecting a series of forcing houses and an orangery at Torville Manor, Lady Southcote was prevailed upon to conduct the company through those buildings, which were her pride and joy.

Into this project Theodosia entered with interest, for she shared, to a limited degree, her brother's passion for natural history. "As long as it is safely contained within glass walls," she laughed, "where I may pick and prune to my heart's content, for there is really nothing so satisfactory as having strawberries in the dead of winter, served upon one's breakfast tray. Jefferson, now, likes to trample through the wilderness in search of such things as mastodon skeletons and Indian burial mounds."

Gallantly, Lord Torville offered an arm to Lady Southcote and an arm to Peerless Theodosia, remarking that if such were the case, Jefferson could tramp all over the grounds of Torville Manor, for the old gaffer had allowed the place to fall into a jungle.

"We do have a barrow on our land," Cynthia told Jefferson as they trailed the others through the conservatories. "The old Celts or Picts or someone used to bury their dead there. Guy and Clare and I used to dig about in it when we were children, but Miss Ipstone soon put a stop to it. I dare say if it were excavated, it could provide some interesting artifacts."

"I should like to look at it someday," Jefferson said shyly. "But what I have always dreamed of beholding is Stonehenge. From everything I have read, *that* is a mystery to behold!"

"Indeed," Cynthia replied, smiling. "Guy and Clare went to see it once, on their way to Oxford. They pronounced it a dead bore, but then, my brothers were never of a truly historical turn of mind."

Jefferson, reaching out to touch a particularly handsome orchid, blooming in the trough beside them, felt his hand inadvertently brush hers. As if he had been burned, he drew away from her, and Cynthia lowered her eyes in a blushing confusion.

Miss Morton-West, trailing the rest of the party with little enthusiasm for growing things, and very aware that her delicate kid slippers were being soaked through on the gravel paths, observed this activity with gloomy disapproval.

"Can't understand it myself," Lieutenant Steyland sighed, pausing to allow Miss Morton-West to catch up with him. "Allowing a couple of hey-go-mad Americans the run of the house. Cousin Albert was always given over to queer notions of propriety, keeping what I can only term most unsuitable company—it's the frivolity of the fashionable life! No proper concern for the Steyland tradition, alas."

"I can quite sympathize with your feelings, Lieutenant Steyland," Miss Morton-West murmured. "Miss Clement seems quite given over to what I may only consider the most depraved conduct. And I may only consider her influence upon the Southcotes to be one of depressing levity." She frowned. "And I do believe that odious mushroom of a brother of hers is making up to Lady Cynthia Southcote in a most improper fashion!"

Theo's laughter pealed through the glass room, joined by the marquess's deep chuckle and Lady Southcote's lighter exclamation of pleasure.

"*Most* improper," the Lieutenant repeated sadly.

Fortunately, the rest of the party remained oblivious of their disapproval, and the marquess spent a pleasurable morning, finding himself on terms of the greatest civility with his hostess.

By the time he had finished his tour, he was begging Lady Southcote to present herself at Torville Manor at her earliest convenience, for no other person in England, he declared, could possibly assist him in restoring his own sadly run-down forcing houses in the very latest scientific mode.

Lady Southcote, pleased to find the marquess such an agreeable and entertaining guest, pressed a basket of strawberries upon him and declared that he must feel free to visit his American friends at any time. The marquess rose to the occasion by pressing her hand to his lips in a manner that made her feel like a deb in first Season again, gave Jefferson a hearty handshake and a promise to take him shooting, subtly complimented Lady Cynthia upon both her beauty and her intellect, and delivered Theo a wink so broad that she must bite her lower lip between her teeth to repress a smile.

"Ah, my Peerless Theo!" The marquess murmured devilishly. "If you run into the fences, you have but to call upon me!"

Theo nodded, pressing his hand in her own with

warmth. "I hope we shall contrive, Albert, but it is good to know that you will stand the friendship!"

The marquess raised one brow eloquently. "I had rather hoped for more, dear Theo—but we have time enough for that! A more loved captive—" His voice trailed away into his lazy smile, and Theo turned her head away to speak to Lieutenant Steyland, apparently oblivious of these hints cast out in her direction.

But Miss Morton-West had observed all of this, and pressed her lips firmly together in disapproval of such flirtatious conduct, adding this scene to her list of Miss Clement's many wrongs.

As the marquess and his cousin rode down the drive, Lady Southcote sighed, her eyes sparkling. "Torville! Here! I dare say that my country season has been made, for the man has only to put in an appearance to cast us all up into the highest fashion. I must admit that I have sadly misjudged that man. Even if he is of the Carleton House set, his manners are very engaging, and not at all puffed up! Why, he is a most civil, charming creature!"

"Albert—Lord Torville—is only odious when he is exquisitely bored, Lady Southcote," Theo said absently, watching the retreating back. "And I am sure that he was not bored here!"

"Dear Theo!" Lady Southcote said. "To think that *you* lured the marquess *here!* An American!" she added naïvely. "Is there no end to your talents, my dear child?"

Theo smiled. "In truth, ma'am, I fear they are quite limited! It is only by chance that Albert and I are acquainted. If I had known that he would move on to become a social lion, I wonder that we all would not have teased him to death over it."

"Known him for ages," Jefferson said, hooking his thumbs into his lapels. "I always thought he was a decent sort of fellow—I never suspected that he was a social out-and-outer!" His tone betrayed a hint of disappointment in his friend that the ladies chose to ignore in their raptures over the fine cut of the marquess's coat.

"And he is not a bit as odious as *some!*" Lady Southcote added.

After supper, the ladies gathered in the long room for tea while Jefferson was left in solitary misery at the table with a bottle of port (which he detested) and the imperious services of Gibney (of whom he was slightly in awe). All through the meal, Lady Southcote had been eyeing her guests in what her daughter could only define as the most speculative manner. Cynthia felt a slight degree of apprehension, for she knew that look quite well, and understood that it meant that her mama had yet another one of her schemes brewing behind her cap. Since Cynthia was as reluctant to participate in entertainments as her mother was expert at their planning and execution, she attempted in vain to distract her parent's thoughts into other directions.

But as soon as the tea tray had arrived, and tea had been poured and passed about, Lady Southcote turned to Theodosia with one of her gentle smiles. "You know, my dear," said this lady kindly, "we have only recently put off black gloves for my son Guy. Of course, when we were in mourning, we could not possibly entertain, but now I think we might perhaps contrive some small entertainment to introduce you and Jefferson to the neighborhood."

Theo lifted the delicate Limoges cup to her lips, with an expression as uneasy as Cynthia's crossing her face.

"Of course," continued Lady Southcote easily, "we shall also contrive to have the marquess present. Will that not set up certain ladies' backs in London this autumn, to find that the marquess came to a simple country ball at Southcote Place? I shall enjoy that immensely." Her eyes sparkled.

"Dear Lady Southcote, I really do not think that it could be considered proper—" Theodosia started, then stopped, her eyes downcast, caught on the horns of a dilemma. On the one hand, she had no wish to obtrude herself or her brother into a society that must at best consider them intruders and enemies, but on the other hand, she had no wish to offend her hostess by rejecting her plans.

"Proper?" Lady Southcote said airily. "Of course it is proper—what could be better than to introduce you to the right sort of people—oh, I assure you, the very best people, no one who would make you uncomfortable or put you to the blush—and of course, snaring the marquess, even in the country, is quite a feat! No more, let us say, than thirty couples, and a champagne remove, one or two very decorous country dances—I dare say I may procure the orchestra from Honiton, or should I send to London for the Pandean Pipes—Gunter's, lobsters in season, of course, and the flowers can come from my own houses—"

Lady Southcote looked to be quite lost in her own plans.

Cynthia leaned over to Theodosia, shaking her head.

"When Mama takes it into her head to entertain, there is nothing you may do to stop her, Theo! She is one of the foremost political hostesses, you know."

Theo bit her lip, nodding. "I see," she said reluctantly. "Lady Southcote, I really do not think that it would be quite such a good idea to ask myself and Jefferson, though—"

Lady Southcote blinked. "But of course it is. What harm could there be in a simple country ball? Perhaps fifty couples and, yes, I think the orchestra from Bath that we had for the Princess Lieven last summer—"

"Mama, we're barely out of black gloves. What will Clare say?" Cynthia ventured, using her last card.

Lady Southcote blinked, displaying that unexpected streak of stubbornness that never failed to amaze her children. "It doesn't fadge!" she said. "A ball we shall have, my dears. Nothing too elaborate, of course— why, I dare say we could not get more than seventy couples together in the country at this season, anyway. And perhaps a very small dinner beforehand, only twenty or thirty at table . . ."

Theodosia cast a look at Cynthia, who gave her a vague, rather unreassuring smile.

Nonetheless, Miss Clement felt a definite trace of uneasiness. To call attention to the plight of herself and her brother was not what she would wish to do. Although she was not of a romantic turn of mind, the image that rose to her brain was that of captive generals paraded in chains through the streets of ancient Rome. Some of this may have betrayed itself upon her countenance, for as Lady Southcote rang for pen and paper with which to start making the first of many lists essential to party planning, she laid a hand on Theodosia's arm. "My dear, I am certain that you will enjoy yourself immensely!" she exclaimed. "And I am sure that there is no need for Clare to know a thing about it, Cynthia! For I am certain that he is still in Vienna! And if he is still in Vienna, we need not trouble ourselves about his approval!"

If Miss Clement was not happy with these arrangements, she was far too well bred to express her opinions in the week that followed. Rather, she devoted her time to reassuring her doubtful brother that it would be a grand evening, not at all out of the way, and stressed that they must at least appear grateful to their hostess for her efforts in their behalf. "For you know that she is doing this to make us feel at home, and there will be many of our old friends there!" Theo said bravely.

Jefferson, who found that his time could be pleasantly divided between perusal of Lord Southcote's excellent library and reading daily installments of Cynthia's novel, together with the singular pleasure of her company, was content, as always, to leave worldly dealings to his sister. Oblivious of anything that did not directly demand his attention, Mr. Clement was content to limit his outings to a fishing expedition with Lord Torville and a morning ride in company with his sister, that gentleman, and Miss Southcote. If Lieutenant Steyland morosely accompanied them, and sometimes they had the honor of Miss Morton-West's company, he barely noticed, for what thoughts he devoted to the world outside of books were largely centered on his blossoming friendship with Miss Clement. Since this blossoming friendship seemed to be largely limited to long and involved discussions of books and literature, Theodosia found herself able to regard the alliance with slightly more complaisance than she had formerly allowed herself. But nonetheless, she kept a sharp eye on the couple.

The marquess was almost a daily visitor to Southcote Place, frequently accompanied by his gray cousin. Since Miss Morton-West's visits to Southcote Place were also conducted with great regularity, and these two elevated people seemed to unite in their silent disapproval of the gaiety of the rest of the company, Theo was able to regard Lieutenant Steyland with slightly less loathing than before. Anyone, she declared privately to Jefferson, who could occupy Miss Morton-West and divert her attention from the sins of Miss Clement and Lady Cynthia should be welcomed openhandedly.

Each morning, the little party would set off for a vigorous ride through the Home Wood. If Torville and Miss Clement chose to gallop on ahead of the more staid members of the party, Theodosia was careful never to allow herself out of their sight, or to spend too much time alone in the company of Torville. She was well aware of his intentions toward her, having known him for many years, and also quite determined that he should have no opportunity to press these attentions upon her, thus forcing her to give him a sharp setdown. At that same time, Theo was well aware that his continued good graces were one of her few weapons in any emergency, and she delicately walked that tightrope between friendship and flirtation with all of her considerable skill, even though privately she felt drained by this constant vigilance.

As much by her own discretion as the invisible

boundaries of her situation did Miss Clement attempt to navigate her course. And if she felt as if she wore invisible chains, at times, she was careful not to betray this feeling to her brother or her hostesses, confining her tensions to the privacy of her own room.

And there, it must be admitted, she sometimes succumbed to tears. But the face she gave this world was placid and self-confident. And such a consummate actress was she that no one suspected the depths of her very real fears of Devonshire Prison or worse. . . .

It said a great deal for Miss Clement's training that Edwina Morton-West was certain that the Southcotes' guest was enjoying herself hugely—perhaps too well, in that young lady's cool eyes. Of a humorless nature, raised on the strictest principles, Miss Morton-West could only interpret Miss Clement's behavior as hoydenish and wholly given over to worldly frivolity. In her view, Theodosia had connived upon Lady Southcote's gentle nature to toss off a grand and far too expensive ball in her honor. Theodosia's defensive relationship with Torville swelled to an outrageous flirtation that bordered upon an out-and-out affair, while Jefferson's growing attachment to Cynthia became, in Edwina's eyes, a sinister attempt to pervert and corrupt a bookish young female into the most unbecoming principles of Emancipated Femininity. Miss Clement's clothes, manners, habits, and attitudes all assumed unladylike and mushroomingly brazen proportions in Miss Morton-West's disapproving eyes.

And her thoughts did not fall upon infertile ground. Lieutenant Steyland had taken it into his head that unless watched very closely, the Clements would attempt to steal such military and state secrets as they could find. That there was no military installation in the district, and that they were thirty miles from the seacoast, that there were absolutely no state secrets to be found at Southcote Place, did not remove this maggot from the Lieutenant's head. The Clements, he felt, were the cause of his disgrace, they were Americans, and therefore they were guilty of espionage, if not by deed, at least by intention. Although Miss Morton-West was sensible enough to realize the absurdity of his beliefs, she did nonetheless encourage him to express his dislike of the Americans, and upon this common ground their friendship prospered well, particularly when it was discovered that their mamas had been bosom-bows in their respective London Seasons.

But it was only when Miss Morton-West, upon arriving at Southcote Place one morning and dismounting from her curricle, was beset by Hester and Gussie in the guise of wild Indians, their small bodies half clothed in makeshift buckskin, their faces painted with watercolors, and feathers from their mama's hats thrust into tangled locks as they emerged from the shubbery and threatened to scalp her, that she decided that Steps had to be taken.

After warding off a bout of strong hysterics with the aid of Lady Southcote, who was further discomposed to discover that her youngest offspring had secured their release from the schoolroom by tying up their governess in the manner Theo had ascribed to the Iroquois Nation, Miss Morton-West watched the number of cases of champagne delivered from Gunter's for the forthcoming ball being loaded into the cellars and took herself home once again to pen an agitated letter to her fiancé.

Enough, after all, was enough, and surely Clare would wish to put an immediate check upon the all-too-lively doings which threatened to overcome the serenity of Southcote Place.

CHAPTER FOUR

The hour was closer to morning than midnight when the hackney carriage discharged its single passenger before Royal Albany Walk.

This gentleman, attired in a severe gray traveling coat with only six capes, picked up his single portmanteau and let himself quietly into his own rooms with his latchkey.

The door swung back on darkness, relieved only by a single guttering candle on the writing table that stood in the main room. In its dim light, he perceived the slumbering figure of his valet, slumped in a chair beside the fireplace, snoring softly.

Correctly interpreting this to mean that Bainbridge had waited up for his master's arrival from Vienna, Lord Claremont Southcote smiled to himself and casually tossed his hat upon the writing desk. He was in the process of undoing his gray onyx buttons when the valet stirred, impelled by some sixth sense, and awakened with a snort.

"My lord!" That middle-aged gentleman's gentleman exclaimed, rising to his feet with every sign of embarrassment at having been caught napping. He pulled his waistcoat down and hastened across the floor to relieve Lord Claremont of his raiment.

"I tried not to wake you, Bainbridge," Clare said ruefully, giving his man a glimpse of his charming, crooked smile.

But Bainbridge was already clucking over the sad state of Lord Claremont's Hessian boots and the travel stains upon his dove-gray coat, regarding his master fondly. "Really, Lord Claremont," he scolded, with all the familiarity of one who had served the Southcote twins since their cradle days, "if you must travel without me, at least you could make sure that you don't let them touch your Hessians in these furrin parts. . . ." With a sigh, he fingered a mysterious stain on the coat, then regarded his master.

Lord Claremont Southcote was not a handsome man. He resembled the earl far too much for that, with the same craggy brow and deep-set eyes, the same tightly drawn mouth and strong chin. But unlike the earl, his gravity could be betrayed by that charming smile he had inherited from his mother. It did not come as often to his face as it had to his brother Guy's rather more handsome countenance, but when it did, it rarely failed to charm the person it was intended for. He was of medium height and dark complexion, but his powerful shoulders required no padding from the redoubtable Weston, and his legs were shown to advantage in his (now sadly stained) buckskin pantaloons. His waving brown hair was cropped into a simple Brutus, and his only ornament was a handsome fob depending from his watchchain. Careless Lord Claremont might be of his dress, and there might be those who would say that his manners were as toplofty and abrupt as his famous father's, but for all of that, he had many friends, particularly among the Corinthians, who knew that a generous heart and a firm loyalty to those who had won his affections lurked behind that cool exterior.

If the laughter came less frequently than ever, and the glimpses of that twisted smile were rarer since the death of Guy Southcote, his character was solid enough that his well-wishers awaited its return in due course with patience and understanding of his grief.

Bainbridge, still clucking over the unfortunate condition of his master's apparel, knelt and gently worked off the offending Hessians. As one foot was freed from its prison, Mr. Southcote sighed and leaned back in his chair, lighting up one of his cigarillos and pressing a hand against his aching head.

"Nothing but one long storm all the way across the channel, y'know, and the coach from Dover was abominable."

"If you had only thought to drop me a line, my lord, I should have sent Tillman on with your chaise," Bainbridge said repressively. "Imagine, wanting to travel on the common stage, as if you were a nobody!"

Claremont wriggled his stockinged toes. "The less attention I attracted, the better it would be! But my mission's accomplished! Gordon now has the dispatches safe in hand, and I daresay that will be enough to back Talleyrand right into the cat's own corner! Bainbridge, never, never trust your dispatches with the military!" He yawned.

"As if I am like to do so, my lord. I will need a tincture to remove this stain. That's a sad business, and no mistake."

Claremont smiled beneath his lashes. "Here I am, Bainbridge, fighting the elements in service of my country, and all you think of is a few paltry stains upon my coat!"

"For them that knows you, my lord, those stains is a disgrace to your profession, to me, and to Mr. Weston! I don't know how many times he has implored me to get you to take better care of your clothes! Time you was in bed. I'll imagine you haven't had a wink of sleep in two nights."

"Or two days, either. That Viennese pastry sits heavily upon my stomach. Gives me nightmares!" He stretched and looked about the room, where the first blue light of dawn was filtering in. "Any news?"

"A letter arrived from Miss Morton-West, my lord," Bainbridge said, brushing doubtfully at Clare's coat. "Walking about Vienna looking like a clerk from a counting-house! Lord Claremont, this is dispatch ink! How am I to remove dispatch ink from bath superfine?"

"You'll manage, I'm sure," Clare yawned, carelessly undoing his cravat and dropping it upon the chair. He picked up the letter on the desk and glanced at the precise, familiar handwriting, then dropped it again. "I'm fagged to death! Bainbridge, I'm to bed, and I intend to sleep for as long as possible! Glorious, wonderful sleep!"

"Very well, my lord," said the valet. "Perhaps, just perhaps, waxed paper ironed very gently . . ."

Lord Claremont Southcote slept heavily into the next day. It was well past evensong when he awakened himself with a murmur and a start, to find himself safe in his own bed.

For a few moments he lay trembling, drenched in sweat, reliving the same scene that had plagued his sleep since Guy's death. In the dream, he was wandering across the battlefield, searching frantically amidst the smoking carnage, looking into the distorted, dead faces of fallen soldiers for that one face—and always, he thought, pressing his fingers into his eyes, it was the same. Beside the twisted wreckage of a cannon, he walked up a small hillock, and there, beside his brother's fallen horse, he gazed with horror into the lifeless face of Guy, dead eyes staring unseeing toward the blackened sky.

Although the dream no longer plagued him with the same intensity it once had, it was still enough to remind Lord Claremont that he was separated from his other half, never to be reunited. And God, how he missed Guy, who had always been able to coax him out of his sullens with a sly jest or a scheme to go out upon the town, just as Clare had been able to gently curb Guy's more dangerous scrapes . . . except that last, foolish charge on a battlefield in Spain.

Feeling somewhat shaken, and definitely not in the best of moods, Clare rang for his tea.

When the tray arrived, Bainbridge had propped Miss Morton-West's letter against the teapot. As Clare dug into his bacon, he studied that precise handwriting without much enthusiasm.

With Guy's death, Clare had known that it was his duty to marry. He had never been much in the petticoat line, for most of the misses presented to his attention each Season seemed to him precisely the sort of dead bores that he was forced to deal with in the course of his diplomatic work. Guy, who had been very much in the petticoat line, had always castigated Miss Morton-West as a prosy bluestocking, but his twin, bereft of his brother's lighter touch, had offered for Edwina because she had been nearest to hand, and in her melancholy manner he believed that he had found some reflection of his own outlook. He had known her all his life, and while he could by no stretch of the imagination say that he loved her, he did respect her air of dignity and her attention to all matters of etiquette, believing that she would make him a complaisant wife and a good hostess.

Brought up in a household managed by two parents whose own arranged marriage was one of mutual tolerance rather than any genuine affection, Clare's rather pragmatic disposition did not incline toward what he considered the emotional excesses of romance. He knew that Edwina did not love him any more than he loved her, and that she had been out two Seasons without receiving any offer her father would consider up to snuff. But Edwina would make him a decent wife, understanding exactly what would be demanded of the future Lady Southcote. And he was sure that she was concerned with the welfare of his family, for her letters still bore what he subconsciously recognized as the traces of the tale-bearing schoolgirl she had once been. But he was able to convince himself that it was all in his own best interests. Since the earl took little interest in the domestic details of his family, it had always fallen to Guy and Clare to keep an eye upon Southcote Place, and in his absence, Edwina had taken it upon herself to be his eyes and ears.

Carelessly, he broke the seal and scanned the crossed and recrossed pages. If he had been expecting no surprises, he was very much mistaken, for the tone of Edwina's letter was very much agitation, and not even the neatness of her pen could disguise her *angst*. As he read the tale Miss Morton-West painted of life at Southcote Place since the arrival of the two Americans his father had foisted upon his mother, his brows rose sharply. He was jolted into repeating certain phrases aloud. "American adventuress . . . mushroom brother—making up to Cynthia! Lady S. giving a grand ball in honor of . . . the marquess of Torville!—How comes that coxcomb into this?—parrots in the schoolroom . . . wild Indians . . ." A faint smile began to play about his lips, then faded into an ominous thundercloud. "Miss Clement riding Guy's horse daily—by God!" His voice rose slightly, and his fist clutched the arm of his chair, but he forced himself to read the letter through once more to be certain that he had caught it all correctly. Crumbling the letter into a ball, he rose from his chair and called loudly for Bainbridge.

The valet's knees shook slightly when he saw his master's face, for he knew that expression well, and knew that it boded ill for someone.

"Pack my cases! And throw in some evening dress! I'm off to Southcote Place immediately!" Clare roared, tearing off his dressing gown. "And tell Tillman to have my phaeton ready at once!" he commanded grimly. "By God, I'll set this situation to rights if I must use a horsewhip! An adventuress indeed!"

CHAPTER FIVE

With two changes and only one ten-minute rest at the Hart and Hare in Salisbury, Clare was able to rein into the long drive at Southcote Place at just a little past two in the morning.

If he had been expecting to rouse up Gibney from a sound sleep, and to stable his own mounts rather than awaken Sexton, he was sadly mistaken once again. And Lord Claremont Southcote was a man who did not like surprises.

The house was ablaze with lights, and, as he reined in his phaeton between a barouche with a ducal crest and a yellow-wheeled high-perch phaeton crowded into the parkway, he heard the gay strains of the latest and most fashionable waltz drifting out through the open French doors of the ballroom and caught sight of several gaily dressed revelers strolling in the gardens by the light of Japanese lanterns.

He tossed his leaders to the post boy and threw orders over his shoulder for their stabling as he ran up the steps.

Gibney himself, magnificent in his best livery and wig, threw open the door, expecting to admit a late-coming guest. "Lord Claremont!" he gasped in surprise as Lord Claremont, travel-stained and thunder-browed, strode past him into the hallway. "Is there aught amiss, my lord, that brings you down from London thus?"

Clare looked about himself at the embankments of flowers. "I should say so! What the devil's the meaning of all this, Gibney? I arrive to find a ball in progress—"

He glanced into the ballroom and mentally estimated that there must be a hundred or more people thronged into that space beneath a pink-striped silk canopy.

"Oh, my lord, it was nothing. You should have seen us earlier this evening. I dare say Her Ladyship entertained five hundred easily tonight—one of her greatest triumphs, for the Prince Regent himself was kind enough to come up from Brighton to put in an appearance to meet Miss Clement, and of course we still have the marquess of Torville—" Gibney's voice was full of pride, but he broke off doubtfully as he looked at Lord Claremont's face.

Clare was shedding his driving cape. "And which one is Miss Clement? That painted jade with the gold lamé shift?"

Gibney peered over his master's shoulder. "Oh, no. Miss Clement would never be so vulgar. That's some relation of Miss Morton-West's, I believe."

Clare's mouth tightened and he craned his neck, looking into the room. "Then by God, which one is this damned adventuress? This Clement chit?"

Gibney cleared his throat. "Miss Clement is a tall young lady in emerald green, my lord."

But Clare could not sort her out from the dancers. With narrowed eyes, he swiftly debated whether or not to confront her directly, in all his dirt, or save his mother embarrassment and change into his evening clothes. The latter did not appeal to his anger as much as the former, but even his manners were not so far below reproach that he would put his own mother to the blush.

He picked up his portmanteau and proceeded up the steps to his room. "Send me hot water, Gibney, and don't bother with a footman. I can dress myself. And Gibney—not a word to Lady Southcote! I dare say she's had enough for a while. I shall handle this situation myself!"

"Situation, my lord?" the butler asked, genuinely puzzled.

But Clare did not hear him.

Lady Southcote had declared that the prevailing vogue for pink silk tents was *terribly nacky*; her ballroom would be decorated solely with flowers of the season, strung on garland chains and bowered into white wicker baskets in every strategic location. The total effect was that of a vast indoor garden, a bit out of the way and quite beautifully unusual, as the many guests exclaimed.

From ten until two, Lady Southcote, her daughter, and her guests were engaged in the reception of guests. If Theodosia had harbored serious doubts about the propriety of introducing two Americans to the *ton*, she found that at least some of her fears were confirmed. A great many people had come, as Jefferson dourly put it, to see the lions. But if these individuals had been expecting to see a couple of raw bumpkins, they were very disappointed. With some urging from Theodosia, Jefferson had rigged himself out in his best evening dress of corbeau superfine, complete to a shade with a cravat tied in the style known as the *trône d'amour* and a pair of black silk stockings, which told the world the young American gentleman was possessed of a good set of calves.

Very high sticklers, such as Miss Morton-West and her haughty mama, might consider Theodosia's gown a trifle too dashing for a young lady of the deb set, but even Edwina, clothed in a modest gown of palest lavender silk, the sleeves and bodice filled with spider-web lace, had to acknowledge that Miss Clement was looking her very best. From the profusion of russet curls dressed *à la Méduse* and threaded through with a thin gold circlet, down to her gold sandals, she was a vision. The dress she had chosen was of watered Italian silk, cut low at the bosom and high in the sleeve, of a delicate hue of Pomona green, ornamented with a gold lamé overslip and gold lamé braid trim at the hem and neckline, caught up with tiny clusters of golden oak leaves to reveal an underskirt of darker green. About her neck Miss Clement had fastened her late mother's emerald chain, and in her delicate ears she wore small hearts of that same precious stone. Since this gown had cost its wearer dear from a very fashionable Paris *modiste,* she was able several times to break conversational ice by discussing, in some detail, the latest styles of that alienated country.

Lady Southcote, if the truth be told, had felt some vague trepidation about the exact style of dress her American guest would choose to adopt. Upon seeing Miss Clement descend the stairs thus attired, she had all but heaved an audible sigh of relief, first that Theo was in the very first stare, and secondly that she did not shine down the lovely Cynthia.

Herself attired in a ball gown of her favorite celestial

blue ornamented with points of delicate Brussels lace, a ruinously expensive India shawl cast negligently over her shoulders, Lady Southcote looked every inch the famous political hostess. Wearing the legendary (and very ugly) Southcote Diamonds, she was able to greet her guests with the greatest amiability and only a very few doubtful glances at her daughter, who had entered into the evening with her customary lack of enthusiasm for all social acitivities.

But not even Theodosia's ensemble could quite take the shine away from such a beauty as Lady Cynthia Southcote. With her golden curls falling about her delicate face from the style known as The Incomparable, the alabaster tint of her complexion set off to perfection by the palest rose crepe of a maiden's ball dress overlaid with a net of silver spiderweb silk gauze, caught at bodice and hem with tiny silver ribbons and hemmed under with a series of delicately embroidered rose-and-silver garlands, her only jewels a set of pearls clasped about her delicate throat, she was enough to take away the breath as she extended one kid-gloved hand to greet her mother's guests.

But as out of sorts as Lady Cynthia had been when her mama's dresser had finished with her toilette, the look on Jefferson's face when he first beheld this vision was quite enough to gratify her out of the sulks. For that look alone, she decided, it had all been worth the trouble.

Lady novelists, after all, must care about their appearance if they were to please their public.

The Marquess of Torville was not known for punctual arrival, nor did he enjoy a reputation for staying above five minutes at any party. As he sauntered into the room, resplendent in his evening dress, greeted Lady Southcote, and raised his quizzing glass to survey Theodosia with critical approval, she laughed and gave him her hand, suddenly knowing that all would be well this evening if he had aught to say about it.

"Peerless Theodosia!" he greeted her, allowing his glass to drop on its riband. "By God, Theo, I shall have to have a waltz with you—no, *two,* and contrive to bring you into fashion! It would amuse me to see every lady of the *ton* aping your American accent and Paris dresses! But see whom I have brought for you!" He turned to indicate, with a wave of his hand, three gentlemen of unmistakable fashion making their addresses to Lady Southcote.

"Bakersfield! Durning! And Fox!" Theodosia exclaimed in delight as she was swamped with exclamations of *"Peerless Theo, by Jove!"* and how did she go on, that *such* a situation must bring her into their midst? Laughing, Theo defended herself from a barrage of questions and sought to single out each gentleman for some word and the promise of at least one dance. Lady Southcote was again vaguely surprised to find her young guest on such intimate terms with such elusive young prizes of the *ton,* and if she allowed herself a smile of satisfaction that each of these eligible gentlemen also seemed stricken with her beautiful daughter upon first glance, it was only the very natural pride of a mama.

Lord Durning, after all, was possessed of considerable estates in the North, Mr. Bakersfield was as rich as Golden Ball, and Lieutenant Fox's connections were most impressive, even to Lady Southcote.

Theo watched fondly as her three old companions

clustered about the beautiful Cynthia, and did not see Jefferson's slightly darkening expression. Torville spoke a few words to him which seemed to relieve that young man's distress, and passed on into the company, leaving Theodosia to face Miss Morton-West and her mama, an imposingly haughty prediction of what Edwina would doubtless become in middle age.

Edwina gave Theodosia two limp fingers in a kid glove and the thinnest of smiles. Her lavender gown of silk and lace was done up in the style her mama considered suitable to maidenly modesty, and she cast a disapproving look at Theo's low neckline. "Remember, Miss Clement, that you must not grant any gentleman more than two dances," she admonished Theo, in an attempt at humor which fell upon that lady in a grimly flat manner.

Theo, however smiled. "Dear me, you must forgive me, for I have granted Torville *three,* and two of them are waltzes!"

She turned away to greet Lieutenant Steyland, and Miss Morton-West merely smiled with silky satisfaction as her mother sniffed, beneath her breath, that Miss Clement was exposing entirely too much of herself for a mere country ball, and were not the decorations entirely too grand?

Having surmounted these obstacles and been able to greet the gloomy Lieutenant Steyland with the appearance of civility, Theodosia gave herself over to her best manners, carrying herself off admirably over the stares of even the most curious.

The presence of the marquess served to draw fire away from Theodosia and Jefferson, particularly since he had made it abundantly clear that they were partic-

94

ular friends of his. Theodosia was amused to discover that their old friend had become the *ne plus ultra* of society, and ruled out the current fashions with a ruthless and dictatorial hand. When he had threatened to bring her into good fashion, it had been no idle boast, for she soon found ladies clamoring to discover her *modiste*, and her dance card was filled to overflowing, simply because he had deigned to single her out for his attentions.

The evening passed most agreeably for her, and she was able to put aside her thoughts for a time and give herself over the pleasures of her friends and admirers. Should Miss Clement express so much as a wish for a lemonade or a glass of champagne, she might choose from several offering hands. If she wished a breath of fresh air in the garden, she moved under what Torville was pleased to describe as a heavy escort, and two young men very nearly came to blows as to which one should retrieve her fan.

If she was aware of Miss Morton-West, sitting in a chair by the wall and regarding her sourly, it did not stop her pleasure in the evening.

She was almost breathless from a lively country dance with young Fox when Torville strode up to her to claim his first waltz.

Spinning about the floor in his arms, lightly held against his corbeau coat, she sighed. "I have not been able to seize a word with you all evening, Albert! I fear you may have brought me too much into fashion!"

Torville gave her his mocking grin, but Theodosia had long ago become impervious to the charms that could melt female hearts in every caste of society. "Believe me, it has been my pleasure. Within a week, they will speak of nothing else but the American Lady in London, and you will see a great number of people who have suddenly decided that they must visit Devon in this season for their health!"

"It is enough that you have lured our old friends out of their town haunts! How very good it is to see them all again, Albert! Tomorrow, we must all ride—it will be very much like old times again, will it not?"

"Not quite," Torville said smoothly. "For you have grown into a lovely female and I—well, you see what I have become."

"Tell me, whatever became of that ancient German baroness you were so fond of?" Theodosia teased him, her eyes sparkling. "I'm quite surprised you have not been snatched up by some wealthy beauty yet! Buckled to a handsome fortune!"

"Lord, Theo, you have a memory like an elephant! And she was not ancient—Gertrude was a widow of all of twenty-seven!" Torville laughed. "She has been replaced so many times in my heart that I have quite forgotten her. I believe she made a very good second marriage to an even older and wealthier count—or was it a prince? Can't keep these Germans straight. But you, Theo, have never been replaced in my heart."

She looked up at him to see if he was teasing, but his eyes were unreadable. "That was all so long ago, Albert," she said lightly. "It was as much calf love as what is going on between my brother and Lady Cynthia Southcote." Light flickered behind her eyes, and her face lit up in a mischievous grin. "Albert, do you feel the slightest partiality for Lady Cynthia? I do wish you did, for it would be wonderful if you would charm her away from my brother. That will not do, you know!"

"What? The Beautiful Intelligence has fixed herself on your brother?" Torville laughed, shaking his head. "Schoolroom misses ain't in my line, Theo, you know that. Stood up with her once at Almack's. D'you know what she talked about? Women's equality to men. At Almack's! I ask you!"

Theo sighed. "I did not think you would suit. But she and Jefferson are much too close, you see, and I must contrive some tactful way to separate them before—well, you may imagine the consequences of my brother declaring himself with Lady Cynthia Southcote! The hanged thing is, Albert, it's moon-calf love, and you know how that can be! If one tried to speak sense to them, it would only push them closer together. So, I am resigned to playing villainess in a high tragedy, always bursting in at the worst moments!"

Torville laughed. "Peerless Theodosia! Do you fear Lord Claremont Southcote shall hear of this and clap your brother into a prison hulk?"

"Exactly," Theo replied seriously. "For, by all accounts, he is a veritable *ogre*. I cannot conceive why Lord Southcote's son should be so, however, but when one considers that female he is engaged to marry—well! I shall say no more upon that head."

"Lord Clare Southcote an ogre? I am not well acquainted with him, but I should hardly castigate him as an ogre, Theo. A rather serious, rather sporting man. Ah, his brother Guy, that was a different matter, however." He told her a most improper story about the late Colonel Southcote and a shared mistress's favors, to which Theo responded with a peal of laughter. "Alas, that Lord Claremont is not more like his brother, then!" Torville finished. "A dull stick, but not an ogre, I trust!"

"Oh, Albert, that cousin of yours has asked Miss Morton-West to stand up with him! Do you think Lord Claremont would approve? I understand that he is a very high stickler—is that the precise phrase I want?"

Albert looked over her shoulder at the couple. "Be good for them both. I say, Peter's driving me mad with his mopes and sullens."

Theo's eyes had a dangerous glint. "I am reminded, Albert. You must stand up with me for two more waltzes! Miss Morton-West has informed me that I may only give two dances to one gentleman or my reputation will be sunk below reproach. But I dare say your credit is good enough to carry me off?"

"Naturally. Always delighted to stand up with you, Theo. But Miss Morton-West is quite right. No more than two dances to a gentleman!"

"Then we shall contrive to change the custom tonight." Theo said firmly. "That woman will not tell *me* how to go on!"

Torville raised his brows questioningly, but said nothing. The waltz ended, and Theodosia was swept away by an eager young man with red hair, leaving Torville standing in the middle of the floor, regarding her with a curious expression on his handsome face. With a slight shrug of shoulder, he took himself off to the card room for a rubber of whist, oblivious of the disappointment of several hopeful females lingering about the ballroom.

When he claimed her hand for the second waltz, Theodosia's mood seemed pensive. She allowed him to swirl her lightly about the room, but her eyes continually searched out the other couples for her brother and Lady Cynthia Southcote.

"If you must disclaim propriety, Theo," Torville suggested gently, catching the drift of her thoughts, "then you must make no claims upon it in others."

"But that is different, Albert!" she exclaimed. "Jefferson is so unwordly. It has always fallen to me to look after him, you see. . . ."

"I know, all too well. Jeff's a good lad, though."

"But this is his first love, and—well, you understand, Albert, that it simply will not do!"

"I have a solution to your problems, Theo," Torville said softly. "You must marry me. Our alliance would certainly render Jefferson and Lady Cynthia Southcote's acceptable, even to the earl."

"But not to my father," Theo said absently, as if she had not caught the last part of his remarks. "He would never approve of such a match, I fear. Jeff is far too young for a wife. And far too naïve to support her in the style to which I believe she would be accustomed."

Torville was about to repeat his proposal when the dance ended and custom demanded that they applaud the orchestra.

Before he could seize her attention again, Theodosia was borne off by Bakersfield for the quadrille, and again he retired to the card room.

It was well after the midnight supper, to which Theodosia went in with Fox on one arm and Durning on the other, before Torville could take up his third waltz.

He had just placed his hand upon her waist, she hers upon his shoulder, when he glanced up and saw an unexpected figure striding across the floor in what he could only castigate as a most shoddily tied cravat. He raised his quizzing glass as this gentleman bore down upon him.

"Lord Claremont Southcote! Unexpected pleasure to see you here! Have you been about all evening, that I should miss you?"

Theodosia froze for a second in his arms, then turned to regard the tall dark man standing over her, glowering at her in a most unpleasant fashion for a few seconds, before his expression flickered into one of vague surprise as he regarded her face.

"Servant, Torville!" Clare said abruptly. "I have just arrived from London. In her haste to extend invitations to this country dance, I seem to have eluded my mother's mind entirely."

"Perhaps it is because Lady Southcote knows of your dislike for social entertainment," Torville said. "Then I take it you have not met your mother's guest, Miss Clement? Miss Clement, may I present Lord Claremont Southcote?"

Theodosia was a tall female, and found it a distinct surprise to look upward so far at a man. But, she conceded, she liked what she saw, despite that glowering expression, for here, she thought, was a man with no pretensions, but all *masculinity,* however unfashionable that might be.

Looking down at Miss Clement, Clare began to feel the first lingering doubts of a long day. Rather than the brass-faced, bold hussy with henna'd hair he had been expecting to encounter, he saw a tall young female with a mop of russet curls and a pair of amused gray eyes that seemed to be reading his thoughts. Sophisticated she might be, for after all she was a diplomat's daughter, but she was every inch a lady and a damned attractive one at that.

Slowly, that charming grin began to spread across his face. "Pleased to meet you, Miss Clement," he said. "I hope you will allow me to cut you out with Torville for the next dance. Host's prerogative, you know."

Theo drew away from Torville with a little sigh at losing her sport. She threw him an amused glance, laying one hand on his arm. "You will accept my apologies, will you not, Albert?"

Torville nodded urbanely. "My pleasure. Although, if you hear a shot in the garden, Southcote, you will know that it is me, blowing my brains out." He raised Theo's hand to his lips, delivered her an odd glance, and strode away.

Theo turned to Clare and held out her hand. "Lord Claremont?" she asked, still smiling at him.

Allowing Clare to lead her in a polonaise, Theo quietly appraised the Ogre. If she had been expecting someone more along the lines of gloomy Lieutenant Steyland, she was pleasantly surprised by the assured gentleman who guided her gently but firmly through the steps of the polonaise, still smiling at her in a most disconcerting fashion.

For his part, Clare had almost forgotten the bruising set-down he had been composing all the way from London. To use such words upon this lady would have been inexcusable and, he thought, unnecessary. "You are not at all what I expected," he said at last in his abrupt manner.

"Nor are you," Theo replied in the same spirit, casting him a look from beneath her lashes. She was rewarded with a slight widening of that wonderful smile.

He noted that the emerald color of her gown reflected in the prisms of her eyes.

"Frankly, from Miss Morton-West's description, I had pictured an entirely different sort of female—" Clare began abruptly, then stopped, the smile dropping from his lips.

"Miss Morton-West's description?" Theo asked, feeling a sudden apprehension.

Clare's expression was definitely more forbidding as he recollected his mission. "My fiancée's letters keep me posted upon the doings of my family," he said stiffly.

"Of course. I had quite forgotten that you were to be offered my congratulations, Lord Claremont." Theo wondered at her own lack of enthusiasm when Miss Morton-West was introduced into the conversation. Certainly she could have thrust some subtle barbs in that direction if she had chosen to do so. Instead she took a deep breath and looked over Lord Claremont's shoulder. "I understand you and Miss Morton-West have some sort of an arrangement to that effect. Miss Morton-West has attempted to instruct me in the proprieties, but I fear that my manners fall sadly below her standards. Before you claimed this dance, I was about to stand up with Torville for a third waltz, you see."

"Yes, Edwina has always been well up on the proprieties," Clare said, wondering why he suddenly found this virtue less attractive than before. Across the room, he caught a glimpse of his fiancée, seated beside her mother, conversing with Lieutenant Steyland. His glance wandered down to the female in his arms, and he could not help but note the contrast between the two women, one so colorless, the other so colorful. He frowned and shook his head, recalling himself abruptly.

Theodosia was humming the tune beneath her breath, apparently caught up in the dance, her eyes half closed, a faint smile playing about her lips. Aware that he was studying her, she looked up at him and smiled questioningly. "And what did Miss Morton-West's description of me amount to?"

Clare shrugged. "Let us simply say that Miss Morton-West's powers of observation are strongly colored by her desire to protect my interests, as she sees them."

Theo nodded. "Quite so," she murmured. "Doubtless Miss Morton-West *writes* in the vein of propriety also."

Clare frowned. Looking up, he beheld his sister in the arms of a tall, gangly young man whose resemblance to Miss Clement proclaimed him to be the odious mushroom of a brother. When he caught the look that passed between Cynthia and Jefferson as they whirled past, he recalled himself abruptly to his mission. That, at least, would *never* do!

Abruptly, Clare stiffened. "Actually, Miss Clement," he said in markedly more formal tones, "I have not come here this evening as one of her suitors—although I am given to understand that you have managed no lack of those!"

Theo bit her lip, feeling her heart sinking slowly. She raised her head and regarded him through narrow eyes, following his glance toward Cynthia and Jefferson with sudden, uneasy comprehension. "Indeed," she replied, and the coolness of her voice was matched enough to his. "I presume this information was also through the courtesy of Miss Morton-West? She seems to have been observing me far more closely than I have been observing myself."

"Edwina—Miss Morton-West—has my interests and the interests of my family at heart," Clare countered, annoyed at the slightly apologetic tone of his own voice. "She has hinted that perhaps you have been overstepping your bounds as a—guest of m'mother's. This ball, for instance! This can hardly have been m'mother's idea—"

Theo flushed. Her eyes sparkled, but her voice was calm. "On the contrary, my lord, I did not push myself forward to this entertainment. Your mother—Lady Southcote—was kind enough to believe that my brother and myself would appreciate a ball in our honor! If you must know the truth, nothing could have been further from my desires than to be—well, I shall say no more, but, Lord Claremont, I assure you, this is not at all what I would have chosen! It cannot help but point out to the world that the Clements are in a most unusual situation! Lady Southcote is a very kind and very generous person, I assure you, but the presence of Lord Torville in the neighborhood was actually the inspiration for this evening's entertainment!"

"And the inspiration for yours, also, to judge by the way you were looking at him while you were dancing, Miss Clement!" Clare said bluntly. "Although what you might see to admire about that fribble of fashion is beyond me! I was under the impression that Thaddeus Clement's children were beyond the illusions of fashion!" She stiffened in his arms, but he inexorably continued. "If you wish to set your cap for a title, Miss Clement, you have done well!"

"And if you think that I should care two snaps of

my fingers for some pompous archaic, antiquated title, you are sadly mistaken, sir! In my country, one rises upon merits of deed, not some accident of birth!"

"*Touché*, Miss Clement," Clare replied grimly. "I see that you spar as well as any diplomat! So, I am wrong when I suggest that you drag m'mother into your schemes of buckling yourself? One for you, ma'am!"

"Thank you. Since you feel such an interest in my affections," Theo said sarcastically, "Perhaps it would interest you to know that Torville is an old friend of the family—and nothing more! But since I am informed that he moves in the highest strata of Society, perhaps I should set my cap for him!"

Clare's brow lowered dangerously, and his grip on Miss Clement's waist tightened slightly, causing her to gasp. "I wish you the best of luck in that direction, ma'am!" He shook his head. "Although what Torville would see in a forward female such as yourself I have not the faintest idea! Tell me, shall American manners become all the crack now? I understand Torville's influence is all-pervasive!"

"Then I must absolutely be in apotheosis, for I have danced with Albert—with Torville twice tonight, all waltzes, and would have danced a third with him, but not for you! Such conduct, Miss Morton-West informs me, will not procure vouchers to Almack's, although why I should wish to go there is well beyond my comprehension!"

Since any desire to attend these rather dull gatherings also eluded Lord Claremont, he was forced to bite back his urge to immediately cast his agreement with her. Despite the dangerous twitching of his lips, he was able to keep his voice even. "This does not conclude the number of bones I am forced to pick with you, Miss Clement! I also understand that you have upset the most excellent Miss Ipstone by introducing vicious birds into the schoolroom?"

Theo's brows rose slightly, and she scanned his face. "The parrots? My brother and I were presented with a pair by the bey when we were small, and when I saw that pair in Plymouth, I could not resist! The most dreadful sailor was mistreating them, and so I purchased them away from him! Certainly Gussie and Hester were happy to have them—they are very lively children, after all, and the sort of people who learn by doing. Were you not ever entertained by pets as a child? I understand that you and your brother were also a lively pair of twins, and continually in and out of scrapes—" She shrugged. "A light hand provides more learning, after all."

"I do not need to listen to your views on education, Miss Clement. Miss Ipstone is an excellent teacher! She has full knowledge of five languages, as well as the pianoforte and the globes! She came to us from the Morton-Wests with the highest recommendations!"

"I dare say," Theo said sweetly.

"The second bone," Clare said quickly, "is far more serious, Miss Clement. I understand that you have countermanded my orders, to ride my brother's horse! That, at least, is inexcusable!"

Miss Clement lowered her eyes and studied her little green slippers moving about the parqueted floor. "There, at least, I have little excuse, Lord Clement," she admitted. "But you msut admit that Thunder is sadly in need of exercise. No one had been on his back in eighteen months, and such treatment of a fine animal is inexcusable! As good as that sailor abusing those poor parrots! If you would care to look at Thunder, I hope you will find him in better condition than he has been for a long time! Would your brother have cared to see such a magnificent beast stalled as a living monument to his memory? Forgive me if I speak too plainly, my lord, but neglect is also a form of abuse."

"Perhaps, but Thunder is not suited to be a lady's mount! You might have killed yourself on him any time this last fortnight, Miss Clement!"

Theo flushed slightly. "Sexton seems to feel that I am capable of handling him. I am not a shy rider, Lord Claremont, and what is considered suitable for a lady's mount bores me to tears!"

"Such behavior may be all the crack among young females in America," Clare replied through clenched teeth. "But I must remind you that you are in England now, and as long as you continue to reside in m'mother's household, you will please conduct yourself as befits a lady and a prison—" He halted abruptly, aware that he had allowed his tongue to run away with him.

"A prisoner, sir?" Miss Clement finished for him. "Yes, say it, then! And have done with it! Do you not think that I am well aware of that fact every waking moment of my life?"

There was something so compelling in the quiet tone of her voice that Clare regretted his lack of tact almost immediately. Although he was ashamed of his hasty speech, he was also aware that his own pride would allow him no apology to this young woman. "As you wish, ma'am!" he said drily, "but I must warn you that whatever your circumstances, such tales of your conduct can only damage your reputation, as well as that of m'mother. And I will not have the Southcote name dragged through the mud!"

"Will you not?" Theo asked tightly. "Then I suggest you consult with Miss Morton-West about her gossiping and with Lady Southcote about what you consider to be my encroachments! I must say, however, that I have some rather strong resentment of being told how to conduct myself by a chit who has never set foot off this little island! As provincial as we Americans must seem to you, I assure you that we offer far less food for scandal than your own sort of people! For, from what Torville has told me, the conduct of your *ton* would be outside of enough in New York or Philadelphia!"

Clare looked as if he would dearly love to wrap his hands about Miss Clement's slender white throat, but at that moment the dance ended, and he was able to stalk away from her without a word.

She stood in the middle of the floor, biting her lip for a second, then snapped her fan. Almost immediately she was surrounded by admirers, begging her hand for the last set being made up. With a great deal of effort, Theodosia composed herself with a smile and placed her hand on Mr. Fox's arm. "I really think it would be advisable for me to have at least one dance with my brother," she said smoothly, gazing up into his adoring eyes. "Billy, could you be so kind as to fetch him for me? I think I saw Lady Cynthia Southcote and Jefferson just slipping out on the balcony for some fresh air."

"Your wish is my command," said Mr. Fox with a

bow to Theodosia, and he scurried off to fulfill his goddess's bidding. Mr. Fox wrote poetry.

Jefferson obviously resented being called away from Lady Cynthia's side by his sister's summons, especially when his rival was none other than the handsome Mr. Fox, who immediately forgot Theodosia when confronted with Cynthia's alabaster beauty. Nonetheless he took his sister's hand and led her onto the floor before confronting her with his anger.

"Theo, I never heard of anything so stuffy as dancing with your own sister," Jefferson complained. "Why, there must be twenty beaux in this room who'd kill to have a quadrille with you!" They separated and rejoined. "Anyway, I'd just taken Cynthia out for a breath of air, and we were about to have a serious talk, when I was cut out by *Fox,* of all people! That's unfair!"

"Jefferson!" Theo cut in angrily. "What do you suppose? Lord Claremont Southcote has posted all the way down here from London to deliver me a bruising set-down! Apparently that Morton-West creature wrote him a letter and castigated us in every sort of vile manner! And he believed it enough to come in like a villain in a very bad Castle Garden play—" Furiously, she recounted her conversation with Lord Claremont. "And so, you see, he believes us to be the worst sort of toadying adventurers! I ask you, Jefferson—oh, my blood boils! I have never been so insulted in my entire life—"

Instead of offering her the sympathy she felt the situation demanded, her brother merely frowned at her. "Oh, now, Theo, don't put yourself up against the ropes! I dare say it looks a trifle strange, and you were very wrong to ride his brother's horse—indeed, Theo, if that's the way you're supposed to conduct yourself here, then I suggest that you compose yourself to be more agreeable to Lord Claremont! After all—"

"After all!" Theo blazed, unbelieving, at her brother. "Are you telling me that you're *siding* with him, after what he said to me?"

Jefferson looked a little uncomfortable. "Well, perhaps he has a point. I mean, Theo, I really wish you wouldn't offend him. After all, he is Cynthia's brother, and if you go about making him mad like that, well, you might cast a rub between Cynthia and me—and I, well, the thing of it is, I'm very fond of Cynthia, and I'd rather you were nice to him, so he doesn't look askance at me. . . ."

Theo stared unbelieving at her brother. "Jefferson!" she exclaimed in dismay. "How could you be so spineless?"

He bristled slightly. "Not spineless, just cautious. I mean, Theo, you can take a bit of the heat, can't you, for my sake? Just be nice to him, that's all. She's the most wonderful girl in the world and I'd hate to have to be dodging her brother—"

"Oh." Theo's voice was tight. "I see where it lies. Oh, Jefferson! You are so young, you don't understand at all. But I tell you, brother dear, that no man may think of me as an adventuress and come off free! We shall see who will win this contest!"

"Theo," Jefferson implored her, but his sister's face was set in that expression he had learned to dread.

Miss Morton-West was far too well bred to betray surprise at the unexpected sight of her fiancé in full evening dress halfway through a ball, but she did lift one brow slightly as Lord Claremont dutifully bent over his prospective mother-in-law's hand before turning to her with what she could only define as *the strangest look.*

"Dear Lord Claremont," Miss Morton-West said as she presented her cheek for his dry kiss, "whatever brings you down to the country on such unexpected notice?"

"Your letter, Edwina," Clare replied in an undertone. "It alarmed me considerably more than you must have intended, for I immediately came down by post expecting to find the house under siege and my mother held prisoner by a couple of American roughnecks."

There was something in his tone of voice that made Miss Morton-West vaguely uneasy. She was about to inquire just what he had meant by that remark when Lady Southcote bustled up to them, peering over Clare's shoulder to ascertain that her eldest son had, indeed, arrived from London.

"Clare! Really!" she said, snapping at his wrist with her fan. "What ever do you mean, simply appearing like this, without so much as a word to your mother? The very least you might have done was to inform Gibney so that I would not spot you halfway across the room and think that Guy's ghost was haunting us!"

"We shall discuss this later, Edwina," Clare murmured, turning to his mother.

Oblivious of his dark look, Lady Southcote immediately began to adjust her son's cravat, still talking, as she delivered him a kiss. "Of course—there, that's better, dearest—I did not mean to imply that you are not welcome in your own household, Clare, but to simply appear out of the blue and in the midst of a ball—and it is a very charming ball, is it not? Have you made your greetings to Lord Torville? I saw, of course, that you had come in and were talking to Edwina, but you must at least make the rounds, and speak your piece, or people will think you dead-witted! Just think, I sent out invitations to five hundred, and received three hundred and eighty-nine acceptances! Is it not the most wonderful thing! I declare, it is quite the most successful gathering I have ever given at Southcote Place!" Her ladyship was clearly in high gig. Her eyes were sparkling and there was a becoming flush to her complexion. Indeed, Clare had not seen his mother so animated since the death of Guy.

"I—I took a sudden fancy to post down to the country. Thought London was intolerably close this time of year, wanted to rusticate for a few days. But I didn't expect to be entertainin' the masses tonight, Mama!"

Lady Southcote's eyelashes fluttered. "I daresay you have not received my letter, then—no, of course, for I thought that Torville might frank it, and then quite forgot to post it. But you are here, and that is what counts! Do you disapprove? Of course, we have visitors from America—children of Thaddeus Clement's, a most embarrassing story, I'm certain that your father must have told you about it—have you met the Clements? A most charming pair—even if they are Americans—and Clare, my love, it has been such a perfect reason to have a ball!"

Clare was not heartless enough to thrust a spoke into his mother's wheel. She was so clearly enjoying her ability to entertain again after the long mourning period that he merely smiled, murmured that he had met Miss Clement, at least, and kept his opinions to himself.

"I trust you have settled in? Good, I knew Gibney would see to you. Really, Clare, it is not at all like you to come without notice—much more like poor dear Guy— Now, my love, you will make the rounds and say whatever is polite to our guests before you stand up with Edwina, will you not? Tomorrow we shall have a comfortable coze, but tonight, my love, we really must see to our guests—Lady Ombersledge! How lovely to see you again!" With a last flutter of her fan, Lady Southcote drifted away to greet yet another guest. Clare smiled after her and shook his head slightly.

"But surely, Clare, you must see why I felt it to be my duty to inform you of the goings-on at Southcote!" Edwina resumed. "Only look at your mother! She is in a most unbecomingly lively state tonight! Why, she even danced!"

"Did she?" Clare smiled, then recalled himself. "Really, Edwina, do you think it your place to point out my mother's conduct? Certainly she may dance if she wishes!"

"Well!" Edwina sniffed. She looked as if she wanted to say more, a great deal more, but at that moment, Lieutenant Steyland approached her.

"Miss Morton-West, you promised me a country dance," he said, casting a doubtful look at Lord Claremont.

"Oh—oh, yes, of course. Lord Claremont, may I present Lieutenant Steyland—Torville's cousin, you see."

Both gentlemen made perfunctory greetings, and Lieutenant Steyland escorted Miss Morton-West onto the floor, leaving Clare to the stiff, disapproving conversation of Lady Morton-West. Nonetheless, he had a slight sense of relief, for he was certain that his temper would not tolerate Edwina's talk of duty and propriety.

Nor was his temper soothed by watching Miss Clement stand up with one young gentleman after another, apparently enjoying herself hugely.

He was glad enough to slip away into the card room for a few rounds of deep basset when Lady Morton-West's attention was elsewhere.

CHAPTER SIX

Several years in the diplomatic service had enabled Lord Claremont to adapt to the habit of dancing all night and still awaken at a reasonable hour in the morning without any loss of energy. When Clare rose at nine o'clock on the morning following the ball, he did, however find that a night's rest put a slightly different perspective on his conduct with Miss Clement. Perhaps, he thought as he attired himself in his riding dress, he had been a trifle hasty with her.

Since he did not expect to see any of the ladies of the house until quite late in the afternoon, he was not surprised when he breakfasted alone in the parlor with his morning paper and the vague noises of a platoon of servants clearing away the night's debris.

At the stable yard, Sexton greeted him cautiously. "You ought to tell us when you're a-comin', Lord Claremont," the elderly groom said as he hobbled forward. "And you ought not to allow the Hart and Hare to fob you off with such cattle, neither."

Clare tossed his gloves from one hand to the other, aware that Sexton was awaiting a stern lecture on the matter of Miss Clement and Thunder. "I suppose I ought to have a look at m'brother's horse—Lord only knows what that female had done to him," he contented himself with saying.

Sexton shook his head. "Can't do that. Miss had him saddled and took 'im out this morning for her ride with the marquess."

"What?" Clare demanded, incredulous. "You let her take that horse out—against my orders?"

Sexton shook his head. "She told the undergroom that you said it was all right with you. Done it afore I could see what was afoot, whilst I was a-havin' of my coffee. Now, my lord, I know what you're thinkin', but it isn't so, it isn't so at all. Miss is right about one thing—that horse needs a rider—it's proper cruel to keep him in his stall, with all the world a-callin' out to him." There was a faint gleam in the old groom's eyes. "'Cept for the skirts and the saddle, she rides like a man! Miss is a neck-or-nothing goer, and pluck to the backbone besides! She handles that horse just as easy as butter, and no mistake!"

Clare opened and closed his mouth, unable to find anything to say to the man who had put him on his first pony. But his brows drew downward in a most alarming fashion and his voice was cold. "We shall say no more upon this head! Having met Miss Clement, I can imagine that she contrives everything to suit herself! Be good enough to saddle my horse!"

"Yes, my lord, but I tell you, there's naught to be worrit about! You have only to see her seat—and the finest pair of hands—"

"Saddle my horse!" Clare repeated, and Sexton scurried away.

Clare, uncertain whether he was more exasperated by Sexton's unprecedented praise of a female or the fact that Theodosia was out on Thunder with Torville, paced the stable yard in a foul temper until his own horse was led out. Swinging himself up into the saddle, he rode off at a gallop down the bridle path through the Home Wood.

He was heading in the direction of Torville Manor when he came upon a skeletal figure mounted on a gray plug, and checked himself long enough to recognize Lieutenant Steyland's gloomy face.

"Good morning, Lord Claremont," that individual said, falling in beside him at a slackened pace.

"Have you seen Miss Clement and Torville?" Clare demanded.

Steyland nodded gloomily, jerking his head to indicate they were farther up the path. "Two of them decided to gallop. *I* do not like to gallop. I'm a man of the sea, myself. Never did like horses all that much. Give me a rolling deck beneath my feet and I'm happy. But, thanks to Miss Clement, I'm landlocked."

Manners forbade Clare to return the answer he would have liked to give Lieutenant Steyland, and manners also forced him to rein in and keep his pace even with that of the gray. But he was beginning to discover that he disliked Lieutenant Steyland even more than his fashionable cousin.

"Can't see it, myself. I'm almost as glad as Miss Morton-West that you've come down here to put a cap to all this foolishness with the Clements. Treatin' these people like guests, when they're crown prisoners! Enemies of England, that's what they are! Ought to be in Devonshire Prison with the other American prisoners of war."

"Perhaps you are right," Clare replied grimly, scanning the woods ahead for some sign of Miss Clement and his horse.

Lieutenant Steyland nodded again. "They ought to be watched, you know. Lord only knows, they could be out spying on our coastal installations. Not to be trusted, the pair of them, him hidin' behind those books all the time and her—well, she's got the entire neighborhood twisted about her little finger! Never saw anything like it in my entire life! I'm glad you're here, Lord Claremont. You will certainly know how to put a stop to all of this—frivolity!"

Clare was about to reply when they rode out of the woods into a clearing surrounding the ruins of an ancient Celtic barrow, some five hundred yards distant. Miss Clement and Torville had just ridden around the circumference of the ancient mound, and for one second, Clare was caught up in admiration of Theodosia's horsewomanship.

Thunder was a giant beast, high-tempered and skittish, but she handled him easily and without exerting too much control. Astride the great bay horse in her magnificent habit, she was indeed a sight to see in the morning light—a proud, fearless woman handling a fine horse with style and grace. For one moment, Clare forgot his quarrels with Theo and simply admired the easy way that she set the horse to a gallop across the clearing towards him, the marquess in close pursuit but no match for her.

She reined in beside him and nodded. "Forgive me!" she said at once. "I know it was wrong—but I—I had my reasons, you see."

Clare allowed himself to laugh. "After that display

of skill, Miss Clement, I would almost be willing to forgive you anything!"

"Ah, Southcote!" Torville called. "I see you have come to join us!" He cantered up easily beside Theodosia. "Well, again Peerless Theo has bested me! That's one guinea I owe you, Theo!"

"I see what your reasons were, Miss Clement," Clare said evenly, almost enjoying the way her face fell in dismay. "Good morning, Torville. On the contrary, I've come to fetch Miss Clement and my horse back home again. Perhaps we shall see you later in the day. Coming, Miss Clement?"

Theo threw him a blazing look, but said nothing. With a few words to Torville, who smiled lazily and nodded, she allowed Lord Claremont to lead her back along the path until they were out of earshot.

"I suppose I deserved that," she admitted reluctantly at last, drawing abreast of him. "But was it so necessary to embarrass me, dragging me home as if I were a child?"

"Since you seem to have as much want of conduct as a child, I suppose it was," Clare said steadily, watching the way her gloved hands handled the reins.

"Ah," Theodosia replied. She looked as if she wanted to say a great deal more, but she was silent for a long time. At last, when she spoke, her voice was low, almost melancholy. "I know that I had no right to take your brother's horse—this morning or at any time this fortnight. But you see, when I am riding, especially when I am riding Thunder, it—well, it allows me to forget—just for a while, you see—that I am a prisoner." She tossed her head. "I dare say it may seem missish and foolish to you, Lord Claremont, but to be confined—to be a stranger among strangers—an enemy—it is not pleasant."

Clare threw her a glance out of the corner of his eye, waiting for her to make some gesture or toss off a joke. But she did not. She merely kept pace with him, her eyes downcast. He thought that he saw a teardrop sparkling on her lashes, but he was not certain.

"So," she concluded, tossing her head back, "my one single act of rebellion has been to steal your brother's horse each morning for a few hours of freedom—I dare say that he feels it as much as I do—rather like one another, we are. Both prisoners in refined circumstance, both undetermined in our fates."

"I see," Clare said with considerably more sympathy. "Does my mother treat you so ill, then?"

"Oh, how can you think such a thing? Lady Southcote has been kindness itself! Every consideration has been given to our feelings—my brother's and my own. She was kind enough to believe that we should enjoy having a ball given in our honor! Last night, my lord, was one of the most agonizing experiences of my life! I felt as if everyone had come to see the lions in the zoo! Oh, I've said too much! Forgive me, for I know that Lady Southcote's intentions were kind, but if it were not for my friends all making an appearance, I should have been ready to sink into the floor!"

"I think I begin to understand, Miss Clement," Clare said softly.

She smiled. "Please do not think upon it! It was but a momentary thing—I have been dreadfully indulgent. I suppose I am feeling the ill effects of too much champagne last night, for ordinarily, you know, I ask no quarter and give none—or so I am told!"

"Peerless Theodosia?" he asked.

She shrugged. "A nickname. We were all together in Germany, you see—" Her voice trailed off and she placed a hand against her forehead. "Nothing really. Just a trivial nickname."

Clare had the feeling that there was something else weighing on Miss Clement's mind, but he did not press the point. Had he known that Torville had repeated his proposal to Miss Clement once again that morning, he might have understood her situation in a better manner.

"You are a capital horsewoman, however," he admitted after a brief silence. "I suppose that if you can handle that nag, you may continue to ride each morning."

Theodosia gave him her best smile. Her face lighted up like a child's, delighted with an unexpected treat. "May I?" she asked. "Thank you! You are very good! You have no idea what these few hours of freedom mean to me."

Clare, who had felt much the same way all through the days of his schooling at Harrow, merely nodded. "And," he said impulsively, "I dare say, while I'm down in the country, we might take out the phaeton! I'm told that I'm a fairly creditable whip. Do you drive, Miss Clement?"

Theo shook her head. "No, that is something that has never come my way. I have admired Miss Morton-West's equipage, however."

"Mine is far more dashing. A high-perch phaeton with yellow wheels. Shall I teach you how to handle a four-in-hand team?"

"Oh, yes!" Theodosia replied. "I would certainly like

that above all things. Then I should become very fashionable, I suppose, and be forced to order my own!"

They both laughed, and they returned to the house in a far better humor than they had started out, each one a little less certain of their first impressions of each other.

Returning into the house by the side door, Theo was just about to draw off her gloves when she and Clare were brought up short by strident sounds from the direction of the morning room.

"My lady! This is not at all what I have been used to in a *gentleman's* house!" Gibney's agitated tones stressed, followed by a sickening sound of breaking glass.

"Oh, dear! Gibney, do something!" Lady Southcote shrieked. "It's on the chandelier!"

"Blow me down! Blow me down!"

Comprehension dawned on Theo's face. "The parrots! Oh, no!" She picked up her skirts and rushed down the corridor, closely followed by Clare.

Hovering in the door of the book room, they were treated to the unprecedented sight of the Southcotes' august butler, stripped to his shirtsleeves, standing on a brocade chair in his stocking feet seeking to remove something from the crystals of the chandelier, while Lady Southcote, a twin gripped firmly in each hand, sought without effect to direct his movements. Below Mr. Gibney's chair, a footman held a pillowcase open as if waiting for something to drop into it.

"Hist, Mr. Gibney! I think you got him!" this stalwart worthy said, and received a quelling look for his pains.

"I hoped it would bite Miss Ipstone!" Gussie said, sniffling.

"Oh, do be quiet!" Lady Southcote exclaimed. "If it were not for you and your games of wild Indians, this would not have happened, and your mama is quite put out with you! Wait until Clare returns and he shall deal with you both!"

"Egad!" Gibney exclaimed, and might have lost his balance if the footman had not steadied his chair. A ball of green feathers emerged from the interior depths of the chandelier and, shrieking "Blow me down," flapped across the room, well above the heads of his hunters, to perch on the edge cornice of a bookcase, where he regarded them all with small beady eyes.

"My lady!" protested Gibney. "This is outside of enough!"

"Oh, Gibney, please do something—it's eating Aristotle!" Lady Southcote cried, releasing the twins to clasp her hands to her cheeks. Gussie and Hester, seeing their chance, bolted for the doorway, but were caught up by their older brother's strong arms.

"Have you been giving your mother trouble?" he asked awfully, but Theo saw a twinkle in his eye. The twins squirmed in his grip, looking suitably guilty.

"We didn't mean to let the bird go, really we didn't!" Hester gasped. "Gussie—"

"Hester's carrying tales!" Gussie bellowed, swinging at his sister.

Clare gave them a slight shake. "I'll deal with you later. Now, go and give Miss Ipstone a headache!"

"We already did!" Gussie cried from the safety of the stairs.

Clare shook his head. "Now, what seems to be the trouble?" he demanded, coming into the room.

"Oh, thank God! Clare is here, Gibney!" Lady Southcote exclaimed. "Now you may get down from that chair."

"I devoutly hope so, ma'am," the butler replied, his dignity seriously impaired. "It is not at all what I am used to in a gentleman's house."

"Shh," Clare said. "This poor bird has come through quite enough for one morning, I think." Slowly, he crossed to the bookcase and held out his hand. "Here, bird. Good bird, no one will hurt you. . . ."

The parrot cocked its head to one side and looked at Clare out of one beady eye, shifting itself from one claw to the other.

Slowly, Clare brought his hand up until it rested against the top of the cornice. He looked at the bird and the bird looked back, uncertain.

While his audience held its collective breath, Clare clucked at the parrot gently. As the nervous bird slowly allowed him to provide a perch on his hand, like a falcon, Theodosia sighed with relief.

Clare handed the bird to the footman, who received it as if it were a hot coal. "There," he said quietly. "I think if you take it upstairs, it will be glad to be back in its cage."

"Blow me down!" the bird mumbled, but it was obviously ready to be borne back to the schoolroom, for it did not stir as the footman carried it away.

"Oh, dear!" Lady Southcote sighed, fanning herself with her handkerchief. "I am so glad you were here, Clare, for Gibney broke a Limoges vase trying to catch that creature!"

"Begging your pardon, ma'am, it was the bird who broke the vase," the butler said, "If there's nothing else . . ."

Lady Southcote hastened to soothe the butler's ruffled dignity. "Oh, no! Nothing at all, Gibney! But do let me dress that dreadful scratch on your hand with something . . . Oh, what we should do without you, I do not know!"

Summoning what remained of his forbidding demeanor, Gibney followed his mistress out of the room, his stately tread only slightly marred by his stockinged feet. "It is not at all what one is used to in a gentleman's house, my lady!" he protested feebly. "In *old* Lord Southcote's day . . ."

The door closed upon the rest of this interesting revelation.

Theo had turned away some moments previously, apparently lost in admiration for the view of the Long Garden to be obtained from the morning-room casements. Her shoulders were shaking, and a gloved hand rose to her face.

Clare shifted uncomfortably. He lifted a hand to place on her shoulder, then allowed it to fall to his side, helpless. He had never, he reflected unhappily, been all that competent with weeping females. "Ah—see here, Miss Clement, it's really not your fault. How were you to know that those two imps would cause so much mischief with a set of dratted birds? I shall have to do something more than merely speak to them this time. . . . That bird-witted female, always claiming a headache exactly when they are at their worst . . . not that I blame her! Not your fault at all, Miss Clement!"

Slowly, she turned to face him. To his surprise, her

eyes were not only dry, but betraying a most roguish sparkle, and the lips half hidden behind her gloved hand were twitching upwards in a smile.

Above all things, Clare most disliked feeling that he had been made a fool. Seeing that Miss Clement was not in deepest consternation, but, conversely, highly amused by the preceding events, his first impulse was to deliver a sharp set-down. But there was something infectious about her droll expression, and yes, dash it, it had been rather a funny scene, old Gibney in his stockings, swatting at a great, ugly bird!

Slowly, his frown turned into a smile, and very soon, Miss Clement and Clare were sharing a discreetly smothered fit of laughter, each one cautioning the other with gestures to keep their voices down lest they offend Gibney even further.

In this excellent spirit, they were very much in charity with one another, so that when Lady Cynthia Southcote ventured to discover all the details of the episode of the parrots, she found Clare upon one chair and Theo upon another, both still giggling over the scene they had just witnessed.

CHAPTER SEVEN

Miss Clement, having attained Lord Claremont's charitable graces, was careful not to do anything that would infuriate him again.

Through the lazy autumn afternoons, she proved herself as adept at assisting Lady Southcote in the choice of dress patterns as she was in entertaining the twins for quite some two hours with more sedate tales of her homeland, or teaching Cynthia the steps of the *polonaise italienne,* the dance craze sweeping the Continent.

But it was Miss Clement's enthusiasm for the genteel game of lawn tennis that seemed to bring the company together at Southcote Place upon almost any afternoon. Having discovered two other players in Miss Morton-West and Lady Cynthia Southcote, Theo pressed first her reluctant brother, then the quizzical marquess into service as a fourth. Since Torville had not played at what that bold Corinthian considered a schoolgirl's sport since his early youth, it took him several days to recapture his skill. Clare, also a redoubtable Corinthian, was at first amused by the marquess's attempts to humor that elusive lady he seemed to be courting. But when Clare had observed the way in which the ladies played, with full intent to win, he was pursuaded to reconsider his opinions, and it was not long before he and Miss Morton-West were hitting the ball to Theodosia and the marquess.

Not unnaturally, the lawn courts soon became the center point of gathering for this set of young people. Even such nonplayers at Lieutenant Steyland and Jefferson Clement, always armed with a book, could be found upon the sidelines on any afternoon, although they were always careful to seat themselves on opposite sides of the court. Lady Southcote and Lady Morton-West often chaperoned these gatherings, seated in comfortable chairs and swathed in as many veils and shawls as both considered necessary to ward off the fatal rays of the sun. That the young people could engage in activity all afternoon and still find the energy to attend as many assemblies, routs, and dinners as the Season offered in the evenings never failed to astonish these worthy ladies.

Indeed, Miss Clement's behavior was, for that halcyon period of time, so sedate and circumspect that even Miss Morton-West was forced to remark upon her fiancé's benign influence upon the Clements.

Sitting on the sidelines watching Theo and Cynthia play the marquess and Clare, she chanced to address her thoughts to Lieutenant Steyland, seated beside her.

His response was characteristic. "It may seem very well, very well, indeed, Miss Morton-West, now that Lord Claremont is here to keep an eye upon that pair," he said in a low, feeling voice, "but mark my words, there is mischief brewing!"

"What ever do you mean?" Miss Morton-West demanded respectfully, for she felt that the staid officer must command expertise in his knowledge of the Clements.

Steyland sighed. "Enemies of the country! Granted far too much freedom, you know! Doubtless they are contriving to gather every sort of knowledge about our coastal defenses and military installations in the West Country, and only waiting for the proper moment to pass this information along to their countrymen!"

Since the Devonshire Riots were still rather unpleasantly fresh to memory, Miss Morton-West pursed her lips thoughtfully. That the coast was thirty miles distant, and that the nearest garrison was twice that distance, did not influence her in the least. A gentleman of such information as her friend Steyland must certainly command respect, she thought, and expressing these sentiments so sympathetically caused the young officer to wonder again how Lord Claremont, so obviously unworthy of the elevated female at his side, had managed to captivate her heart.

Indeed, Miss Morton-West could not help but contrast the gratifying sentiments of Steyland rather unfavorably with those of her fiancé when she ventured to express these opinions to Lord Claremont.

Clare, dabbing at his perspiring face with a kerchief, a great deal of his attention given over to the challenge match between Miss Clement and the marquess then in progress on the court, merely shrugged. "Spies?" he asked in a low voice, his eyes following the progress of the ball from one racquet to the other. "The Clements? Edwina, doing it a bit too brown! I think your good friend the lieutenant is almost as large a nodcock as Jefferson Clement. In fact, more than poor Jeff, now that I think upon it! Champion shot, Miss Clement!"

he called. "And indeed, Edwina, why should Miss Clement not conduct herself with propriety? You must remember that she is more used to the ways of government and international circles than those of the West Country. Perhaps her manners might seem a trifle generous to one brought up within the confines of our set, but you might do well to observe how she goes on, Edwina, for soon you will be called upon to move in those circles, you know." To take the edge off this mild setdown, Clare placed a fond hand upon Edwina's shoulder, but not even this playful gesture could take the sting out of his reproof, for no female likes to be compared to another, particularly if she feels that the other lady is taking the shine out of her consequence. Edwina had far too much sense of her own position to entertain the idea that Miss Clement was a possible rival for Clare's affections, but she was annoyed enough to find more pressing affairs at the Grange for quite some days, not entirely to the displeasure of the inhabitants of Southcote Place. The target of her pique, unfortunately, was happily oblivious of this reproof, for he was soon engaged in showing Theodosia how to handle the reins of his famous phaeton.

Here, at least, he knew himself to be without peer, even against the marquess, and he was gratified to find that Theodosia was a quick study who would not, like his sister, put him out of patience with missish fears of overturning the percariously high-slung vehicle, nor, like Miss Morton-West, be far too aware of her own dignity to be put to the blush if she made a mistake.

If anything, Miss Clement was perhaps a bit too reckless for her own good, for she managed to overturn the curricle in the drive, spilling them both out upon the gravel.

After assuring himself that she had escaped with only a few scratches upon her hands and a rent in her habit, Clare delivered himself of a blistering reproof upon what he castigated as Theodosia's ham-handedness in not checking her leader.

"That was the most bird-witted stunt I have seen in some time!" Clare said frankly, engaged in calming down the skittish team. "I certainly told you twice that you must rein in, and keep your ribands close to your chest, when you wish to take a sharp turn!"

Theo pushed a strand of hair away from her face and wiped a handkerchief across one bleeding palm. She was more shaken by the fall than she cared to admit, and to be heaped with abuse for an unintentional mistake that Lord Claremont (she thought) could have made as easily as she had seemed vastly unfair.

"If I were a man, Lord Claremont, I should call you out! Indeed, if my pistol had not been commandeered away from me, I would be strongly tempted to do so anyway!" Angrily, she brushed at her skirts with one gloved hand.

This pronouncement had the effect of checking Clare in midsentence. He ran a hand across the leader's back, eying Miss Clement speculatively. "Your pistol?" He asked with some astonishment. "Miss Clement—"

Theo removed her dashing little green velvet shako hat and shook out the plume, tilting it down over one eye. "Of course I have—had a pistol. It was quite lovely, too, for my father had it made up by a Florentine gunsmith to my requirements, with silver scribing and a mother-of-pearl stock." She sighed regretfully. "But of course, when one is taken prisoner, you know, one must surrender one's weapons, which I do not think Father would have liked at all, for he was always most strict that I carry it when traveling in strange places. Bandits and so forth, you know." The faintest smile flickered across her lips, and she lowered her head. "It fits inside my muff," she added regretfully.

Clare was so amazed that his mother's guest knew how to use a weapon that he could only stare a moment at her. Slowly, a smile traced across his face, and he thrust the reins into the hands of Sexton, who had come running as fast as his ancient legs could carry him from the stable yard at the first sign of the accident.

"It happens that I have a pair of Mantons in the gun room, Miss Clement," he said in a voice redolent of mischief. "Would you care to test them out on the range? We could set up targets."

Theo met his eye, torn between militant anger and a genuine desire to try out a sort of gun of which she had heard many good things. "Of course," she replied evenly. "Five hundred paces, and single shot? For you know that my father put me to range until I could pick the eye out of a squirrel on a stump at that pace."

"Mr. Clement seems to have provided for every emergency in your education," Clare replied with some sarcasm.

Theo shrugged, picking up the skirts of her habit.

When Lord Claremont and Miss Clement returned to the house two hours later, the gentleman was shaking his head and the lady's face had a certain rather immodest cast.

Lady Southcote looked up from her tatting. "Good Lord, Theo," she expostulated. "Was that you and Clare out there?"

Miss Clement nodded. "Lord Claremont was anxious that I be able to prove to him that I could handle a pistol with more skill than I can handle his team," she murmured modestly. "I hope that I have proved my skill to his satisfaction."

Her Ladyship shook her head. "Pistols . . . dear me! It is not quite what one would expect, is it? But I suppose you have been in some most unusual situations, have you not?" she hastened to add diplomatirally.

Theodosia nodded, glancing at the clock. "Oh, the hour is quite quarter-past! Are we not to attend the Assembly tonight, ma'am? I must instantly dress for dinner, and see to these scratches on my hands! I shall be wearing gloves for a week!"

Clare watched her retreating back with approval. "A regular dash, Mama! Miss Clement's pluck to the backbone and no mistake! She shows not a trace of *edging*, and she'll face down anything that comes in her way! And she is besides, a crack shot! If you could have seen her take that curve in the Honiton Road— an inch to spare over the Bristol Mail, and she didn't flinch her leaders!" He smiled and shook his head. "If she were a man, I'd take her to Manton's shooting galleries and give her headway! Like to see her put some of those town bucks to the blush! It makes one almost wish that the hunting season were not so far away, for I'd like to see her bag a few quail!"

"Quite so." Lady Southcote blinked, watching one of her son's rare charming smiles flicker across his face as he thrust his hands deep into the pockets of his olive riding coat, staring in the direction of Miss Clement's departure. Until that moment, Clare had always professed a great dislike for what he castigated as *sporting females,* considering such skills as decidedly unfeminine and unladylike. Indeed, Lady Southcote collected, until that moment, he had always declared that he had offered for Edwina Morton-West precisely because she held an aversion to anything but the mildest and most acceptable forms of female exercise.

But Lady Southcote was wise enough to keep these thoughts to herself, merely adjuring her son to think of the time, for he could not possibly sit down to dinner in all his dirt when they were expecting not only the marquess but Lord and Lady Ombersley to dinner.

Clare immediately frowned, pulling his dark brows down alarmingly. "What, that coxcomb?" he mumbled.

Lady Southcote's brows went up as far as her son's had descended. "I hardly think that Mitchell Ombersley is precisely a coxcomb, my love," she said mildly.

"Not him—fustian! Torville! I dare say we've had enough of him pressing Miss Clement to hang in his pocket! When we go down to London for the Season, I suppose we shall never have him out of the house!"

With that remark, Clare took himself off to his chambers, leaving Lady Southcote to some very startling thoughts indeed.

The presence of Mr. and Miss Clement at the Assemblies was no longer any cause for comment, even among the most vulgar gossips.

But the marked way in which the Marquess of Torville stood up at this decidedly tame gathering with the dashing Miss Clement had long ago caused certain entries to be made in the betting books at White's, and even his own sister had remarked that she thought Torville in the buckling mood at last.

Tonight Miss Clement looked particularly fetching in a silken crepe gown of ivory, overlaid with a figured net half-skirt of tangerine, her bishoped sleeves slashed very dashingly to the wrist to expose silk figures in that same hue of orange, her feet shod in neat kid slippers of cream and a morocco leather reticule slung over one arm. Her hair was dressed in the style known as the Aphrodite, and pinned with a single gold arrow, and her only jewelry was a wrought-gold necklet resting against her olive skin.

Her beauty, matched with the marquess's slender elegance, set off by a corbeau coat of bath superfine that could only have been executed by Weston, his cravat the envy of lesser mortals for the perfection of his unique style, which he was pleased to call the Devil's Own, his locks pomaded and glistening beneath the light of the candles, caused even the most envious of damsels to admit that they were a handsome couple as they swirled across the floor in the strains of the waltz.

"Well, Peerless Theodosia," her friend said in his lazy voice, "I begin to think that my strategic remove from the lists is in order. Absence, I have heard it said, makes the heart grow fonder."

"What, Albert, you are not deserting us?" Theodosia asked in some alarm.

The marquess's lids drooped over his eyes. "Theo, Theo! You have quite wounded my pride, you know," he said lightly. "For I am not used to being cast aside for a rough fellow with no graces to his name! Trust you to put me in my place, you wretched American female!"

Theo looked quite puzzled. "What ever do you mean, Albert?" she demanded in genuine astonishment.

"Oh, nothing! Nothing at all, dear Theo! Simply that after dogs' ages of being lionized as a Marriage-Mart Prize, I have finally been made aware of my hubris, dear girl! Time enough I was back upon the Town, anyway. The Season's starting up, you know, and London's filling with company."

"You are deserting me, Albert!" Theo accused. "That is quite vexing of you, when you know that I depend upon you to keep me from utter social ruin by your credit!"

Torville shrugged. "I dare say that you may carry yourself off without me now, Theodosia! Matters seems well in hand. But, my girl, should you find yourself up in the boughs, or in any way hipped by that Ajax's temper, you have only to apply to me instantly for relief. My offer still stands, you know," he added gently.

Theo nodded, not knowing where to look. "I—I quite understand that, at least! And, Albert, I appreciate your feelings, even if I can no longer return them. Five years ago—but that was quite different, you know. We were both children. . . ."

"Would that I could say that I never forgot you in all that time, Theo! But you have grown up so admirably well—you are the only female of my aquaintance whom I do not find to be a dead bore, Theodosia. Whatever else, I sure that you and I would have contrived to set the world by the ears! No matter! If Lady

Southcote decides to repair to Town for the Little Season, you must allow me to make you the rage, no matter what!" His eyes narrowed. "It would give me a great deal of pleasure to watch the mad scramble to embrace all things American, to see Peerless Theodosia cutting a dash in that *ton!*"

Theo smiled. "And you know how very uncomfortable I should be. Depend upon it, I should be bored within a fortnight, and find some way to disgrace us both entirely with one of my dreadful tangles!"

Torville inclined his head to the wisdom of this remark. "Perhaps so, perhaps so! But this is one tangle, Theo, I leave for you to unravel yourself! And I have not the faintest doubt that you *will* unravel it somehow, once you know your own heart! I wonder, you know, if that overbearing, ungainly wretch knows how little he deserves a female like you?"

"Albert, what fustian are you talking? What overbearing, ungainly wretch?" Theo demanded, genuinely puzzled.

Torville smiled. "Don't pretend you don't know, Theo! It's as plain as a pikestaff whenever you two are together that—well!"

"Lord Claremont? Albert, you are foxed!" Theodosia said in a voice so full of honest indignation as to discourage the marquess from saying anything further. "Besides," she added firmly, "not only do I find Lord Claremont to be a bad-tempered tyrant with a short stick, but he is also engaged to Miss Morton-West! Silly notion for *you* of all people to take!"

"Methinks the lady doth protest *too much!*" the marquess murmured under his breath. But, when the dance was ended, he bent over Theodosia's hand in such a way as to make interested observers believe that she must have accepted his offer. What female would not?

Lord Claremont, for one, did, and wondered at his own feelings of revulsion. If Miss Clement chose to throw her cap at that caper-witted beau, what business of it was his? The sooner some arrangement could be made, the sooner Miss Clement and her brother would be removed from his mother's household, and the sooner he could fix a date with Edwina. And doubtless they should suit together very well! he thought firmly.

"Claremont! My foot!" Miss Morton-West whispered gently.

He pulled himself back to his dance partner with effort. "Apologize, Edwina! My thoughts were elsewhere, I fear!"

Miss Morton-West nodded and gave him a thin smile.

Across the room, Lieutenant Steyland watched Miss Morton-West's discomfort with a sigh, plunged into the deepest gloom when he watched her in the figures of the waltz with Lord Claremont. Of course, he himself did not approve of the waltz, nor of so refined a female as Miss Morton-West engaging in the dance, but what was condoned by the lofty patronesses of Almack's must surely be acceptable to Miss Morton-West, if only with her affianced husband. He sighed again, wishing for all the world to exchange places with Lord Claremont, and found some measure of comfort in contriving a dozen ways to blame the impossible situation upon the Clements.

It was a little past midnight when Clare saw his fiancée and her mother to their carriage and returned to the ballroom.

Almost compulsively, his eye sought out Miss Clement. He caught a glimpse of that lady surrounded by her ubiquitous admirers, and felt some unnamed and unaccustomed emotion flicker through his breast.

He was about to join that throng when he felt a tug at his sleeve and turned to see Lieutenant Steyland at his elbow.

"I hope you will pardon me, sir, if I venture to drop a word in your ear," Steyland said in melancholy tones.

Clare's brows drew down. "In what way may I be of assistance?" His tone implied that his words were only a politeness, for Clare had decided that he liked the marquess's cousin even less than Torville, and for far better reasons.

Steyland glanced around, then drew closer to the diplomat. "It's about the Clements," he whispered.

Clare's brows drew together. "The Clements," he repeated tonelessly.

Steyland nodded. "I thought perhaps it might be wise to warn you that they are up to no good," he said confidentially.

"No good?" Clare repeated.

"Espionage," Steyland said firmly. He licked his lips.

"What?" Clare asked in severe accents.

"It is my opinion that that pair are gathering information to pass on to their American friends."

Clare was torn between an urge to plant this whey-faced officer a noble facer and a strong desire to laugh.

"Well, depend upon it, there are spies everywhere. But I am certain that the Clements are somehow plotting to gather information on our military garrisons and coastal defenses in the West Country." The lieutenant nodded again, rather more vigorously. "I have been watching them both very very carefully. They are, after all, enemies of our country, sir, and at the first opportunity, I plan to lay information against them. Since you are with the F.O., I thought, of course, that you might have noticed anything suspicious about them, some small clue or other that might assist me in catching them red-handed with state secrets."

Clare regarded the somber officer with loathing, coupled with disbelief. "Are you quite serious?" he demanded. "That sir, is the most harebrained, corkheaded notion I have heard in quite some time. How do you think that the Clements are acquiring these secrets? Surely it must be with some supernatural effort, since Southcote Place is woefully devoid of any sort of activity of that nature, and the Clements have no access to any of the garrisons or fencibles in the area."

Lieutenant Steyland looked slightly defeated. "Well, all you have to do is give them half a chance, and I'm sure that they will find a way to—"

"Sir, I find your ideas not only those of a nodcock, but also highly improper." Clare's voice was steely. "I shall choose to believe that you are a trifle foxed; otherwise, sir, I might be forced to call you out! Before, sir, I might have been forced to consider you merely a fool; now I am convinced that you are a madman!"

And with those words, Clare strode away.

Miss Clement was still engaged in conversation with her friends. As Clare approached the group, he encountered the amused eye of the marquess.

"Talkin' to my cousin, Southcote?" that gentleman drawled lazily. "You have my sympathies."

Clare shrugged his shoulders within the confines of his coat. "Steyland does seem to have quite a few bees in his bonnet," he admitted.

The marquess nodded. "His father was the same way, y'know. I understand that m'aunt was forced to hire a strong valet to attend him toward the end. But that, I think, was more due to blue ruin than madness. M'cousin's simply a fool like his mother. That's why he's managed to suceed so well in the military."

"Doubtless," Clare replied airily. "But you ought to keep an eye on him, Torville. Someone might take him seriously one of these fine days!"

Torville bowed in acknowledgment.

"Miss Clement," Clare said, smiling at Theodosia, "I believe you have promised me this next dance?"

Miss Clement bestowed a smile upon poor Mr. Fox and a word to Lord Durning.

She put her hand in the crook of Lord Claremont's arm and gave her demi-train an expert kick, looping it up over her arm. "They are making up a waltz," she teased him, and Clare gave her one of his charming smiles.

"All the better!" he said, taking her into his arms.

Theodosia looked up into his face, wondering why she felt so happily safe in his arms, and at the same time so very unhappy. Her smile grew a trifle strained as she suddenly understood the impact of Torville's words.

But Clare was not thinking along those lines, as he gave himself over to the pleasure of dancing with Theodosia, who was so graceful and so enjoyable to dance with. It must be admitted that he wondered why Miss Morton-West could not dance so well with a man's arm about her waist, and why he had found the art of dancing to be a duty rather than a pleasure until he met Miss Clement.

But he did notice her tension despite her attempt to conceal it behind her expression. "Hypped?" he asked. "Would you care to stroll on the terrace? This room is dashed hot, you know! Perhaps a glass of arrack punch would revive you."

Theo, who would have liked nothing better than to stroll on the moonlit terrace with Lord Claremont, shook her head. "Oh, no! If I drink another glass of arrack, I think I shall float away!" Exerting all her concentration, she focused her eyes on a spot just above Lord Claremont's right brow, and tried to make commonplace conversation. "Does not the hunting season start soon?" she asked.

"In a very few weeks. Will you hunt with us? This is humbug country, you know. I wish that I could take you to my box at Melton—there, I promise, you would see some good sport, Miss Clement! However, if you should like it, we may be able to have an afternoon or two of grouse shooting. I think I could promise you something a little better. But of course, in America, you must have better gunning than we could imagine on our little island."

"Oh, yes! On Long Island, my father keeps a lodge, and we were used to repair there to hunt for ducks and geese. Prime sport, I assure you, but very cold!" A trace of a frown crossed her face, and for one single instant, she dropped her guard. "Sometimes, you know,

I think of home and . . . well! Let us say no more about it!"

"You are a brave female!" Clare said admiringly. "I had some news from London today. The treaty negotations in Ghent proceed apace. Your father is pressing nobly for certain points of trade access, and my father is seconding his proposals."

"Do you hear how Father is? His gout sometimes acts up, you know," she said wistfully.

"My father assures me that he is well, and that he sends his love to you and your brother, and has not the least *angst* as to your welfare. He assured my father that you are complete to a shade and well able to handle any situation you might find yourself in!"

The irony in her smile was lost on Clare. Thinking that her wistful expression was due more to homesickness than any other cause, he strove to cheer her by telling her of his conversation with Lieutenant Steyland.

Theodosia's laughter was a trifle forced. "And what do you think? Should you put a guard on our rooms lest we sneak about at night and pry open the dispatch boxes?" she asked with rather more bitterness than he had expected.

"Coming it a bit too brown, Miss Clement! You've given your *parole*, and there is no reason to doubt your word. Well, this will soon be over, and you shall be free to go on your way, with only a tale of adventure left to tell your grandchildren!"

"Yes," Theodosia said in a small voice.

That night, Jefferson came into his sister's room. "I say, Theo! That was a capital entertainment—what's

143

the matter with you?" he asked, staring at his sister, sitting on the covers of her bed, a handkerchief twisted up in one hand and unaccustomed tears rolling down her face. Vague fears assailed her brother, and he frowned, for Theodosia *never* cried.

She strove to pull herself together and smile through her tears, for Jefferson must not have to shoulder her burdens. "Oh—oh, nothing, Jeff! I assure you. It is merely a touch of homesickness that overcame me for a second." She dabbed at her eyes with the balled-up handkerchief and adjusted the folds of her white muslin nightdress, patting the bed. "Do sit down and tell me all about your evening. Did you truly enjoy yourself?"

It was not in Jefferson's nature to worry too much about the intricacies of female emotion. Though Theo was rarely cast down, she was, after all a woman, and subject to mysterious and unaccountable emotions. So, without ado, he deposited himself on the four-poster and regaled her with tales of his luck at penny whist with young Fox and Mr. Durning.

If Theo only listened with half an ear, if she stared morosely out the window at the cold November night, biting her lip and frowning, he did not notice.

But when he had bid his sister a careless good night, yawning and saying that he would see her in the morning, she did not snuff out her candle and pull the comforters up around her head. Rather, she continued to sit on the edge of the bed, kneading the sodden linen in her hand, staring into nothingness. "I must not, I cannot!" she repeated over and over again to herself. "It does not bear thinking about!"

CHAPTER EIGHT

The next day Miss Clement seemed more herself, and there was nothing in her demeanor to suggest that she had passed a most miserable night.

If her behavior toward Lord Claremont was slightly cooler, as if she had erected an invisible barrier against further intimacy between them than that required of two people domiciled in the same household, he was too busy to notice, for that morning he received an urgent summons from Lord Clarke at the F.O., and was forced to post immediately back to London.

Theo could not help but feel a sense of relief, and if she arose each morning and immediately recalled the emptiness of the day, despite a succession of rout-parties, assemblies, dinners, and expeditions to various towns and historical sights in the neighborhood all provided for her entertainment, if she threw herself into these expeditions with fierce concentration and a gaiety that only she knew was forced, no one was the wiser to her puzzling unhappiness.

Miss Clement had not been upon the world for the greater part of her life without experiencing some flirtations and even once or twice forming *tendres* for certain gentlemen. But never before had she felt any emotion quite like this, and it surprised as much as it frightened her.

"Totally ineligible!" she told her mirror as she brushed out her hair with swift, savage strokes. "He is tyrannical, overbearing, and without grace or manners! And he is engaged to another female!" Brutally, she yanked a knot out of her curls and winced. The face that stared back at her was hollow-eyed. "Your father would not approve at all!" she told herself. "You have always prided yourself on having a great deal of common sense, Theo! Now put that common sense to use! You know that it would never work out—you should be at blows within the space of a twelvemonth, you know, and it would never do!" She seemed to collapse into herself. Her shoulders slumped, and she rested her chin in her hands. "No, why could you not—prefer Albert? He certainly has far more to offer you than—than the other! Manners, charm, address, style—every consideration." The face in the mirror could only stare back. "Oh, wretched! Why is it that I can solve everyone's problems except my own? If Hester breaks her favorite doll, I can repair it. If Cynthia is a trifle awkward at the *polonaise,* I can teach her to go through the steps. If Lady Southcote wants to choose a dress pattern, I can tell her which one I think would suit her best. If Jefferson's heart seems to much engaged, I can disentangle him by diverting his mind. If Father's gout acts up, I can make a hot posset—but this—this is one time that I have stepped too far."

She threw the silver brush down upon the dressing table. "Oh, what a wretched tangle!" she cried.

*　　*　　*

Clare Southcote was not an introspective man, but for the first time since the death of his twin, he was aware of some new sense of life within himself. His friends commented that laughter rose more readily to his lips than for some time previously, and once more he was to be seen in his clubs amongst his cronies.

"Something happened down in Devon to change his tune," Bainbridge told his cronies at the Bull and Hare over a glass of heavy wet, shaking his head wisely. "And I don't doubt that it has to do with the American Lady, for you may depend upon it, he's mentioned her name more nor once when himself was asleep, or just daydreaming off over his papers, which, you mark me, he ain't much in the way of doing." That worthy shook his head. "And, from what I hear, the American Lady's far more in his style than that suet-faced female he's gone and got hisself hitched to marry. . . ." He sighed.

Indeed, Theodosia's repute had spread into London, for many returning for the Season from the West Country were swift to remark upon the Marquess of Torville's marked attentions toward the mysterious Original at Southcote Place. That notable gentleman's return to Town was seen by many as a way of preparing his mansion on Grosvenor Square to receive a future mistress, and more than one hopeful damsel who had been the object of his flirts was cast into deepest gloom upon hearing this latest *on-dit*. All the *ton* was agog for news of this female—and an American yet, without proper family connections or title! who would seem to have effortlessly captured the most elusive prize on the marriage mart. The stakes entered upon the betting books at White's were doubled and tripled, but the Marquess himself would only give his lazy smile and a slight shake of his head when questioned directly, discouraging all questions with a raised eyebrow. Since there were few bold enough to risk his ill will, however, the rumors grew in size and speculation out of all proportion.

Clare's business with the Foreign Office fully occupied most of his days, and since his evenings were spent in the convivial company of his Corinthian friends rather than in the ballrooms and salons of the hostesses of the *ton,* it was quite three weeks before he heard the latest *on-dit.*

He had finished off a long day of paperwork with a look-in at Jackson's Boxing Saloon, where he had enjoyed a few rounds with Mr. Jackson himself, when he was accosted by none other than poor Mr. Fox in the changing rooms.

Mr. Fox was rather fresh upon the town, and had still not developed the discretionary polish of his more sophisticated friends. After complimenting Clare upon his prowess in the ring, the young gentleman, hoping to impress his acquaintance with his knowledge, inquired after Miss Clement's marriage plans.

"I say, she must be fixing up a trousseau about this time. Shouldn't wonder if your mother were to bring her into London for her clothes. Everyone is dying to get a look at Theo, you know," Mr. Fox said casually.

"Trousseau?" Clare asked. "Miss Clement we speak of, do we not?"

Fox frowned, as much in apprehension of Lord Claremont's tones as his own puzzlement that that gentleman should not be intimate with his house guest's plans. "Well, it's all over town that she's accepted Torville's suit, you know, and quite a to-do there's been about it. Of course, we who know Peerless Theodosia aren't a bit surprised that she and Torville are making a go of it—a fine match, don't you think? But, as I say, it's the very latest *on-dit*—have you not seen the wager books at White's? The odds lower daily. . . ."

"I see," Clare replied coldly, experiencing some quite novel emotions which he strove to conceal. "No, I was not informed of Miss Clement's plans."

Mr. Fox gave him a strange look, but was wise enough not to say anything, but he did note that in Lord Claremont's second go-round with Mr. Jackson, his fighting style was rather more furious than previously, as if he were boxing in earnest.

Indeed, Clare himself was at a loss to explain his own behavior. Why should it bother him that Miss Clement had accepted Torville's suit? Certainly the fashionable marquess was just the sort of man that she would be expected to prefer, and his attentions to her had been most flattering. If he suddenly found himself reading over the same sentence in a dispatch two or three times without comprehending one word of it, and gritting his teeth at the thought of Miss Clement and the Marquess of Torville going to the altar, such unwonted conduct on his own part only served to plunge him further into one of his black moods. If he scanned Edwina's dutiful letters for some news of this development and somehow blithely ignored her continued references to the wise precepts of Lieutenant Steyland upon this or that matter, it was without a conscious sense of guilt. Somehow, he managed to rationalize his cool anger with the thought that it was his duty, as Thaddeus Clement's deputy in the matter of his children, to prevent Miss Clement from forming any alliance without her father's consent and knowledge. Even though he was perfectly aware that the marquess was a long-standing intimate of the Clement family, and that Mr. Clement seemed to be exactly the sort of cavalier, modern parent who would expect his headstrong daughter to choose her own husband, Clare still was able to convince himself that a visit to Devon was definitely in order at the earliest possible moment. Though he had no very clear idea of what he would say to Miss Clement, or indeed, precisely how he might contrive to convince her not to accept the marquess's suit, at least until the declaration of peace and the return of her father, he managed to convince himself that his duty lay in that direction.

If anyone had been bold enough to suggest to Clare that his true motivations were rather more selfish, and much more concerned with his own feelings for Miss Clement, he would have denied it completely and delivered himself of a pressing set-down. After all, he was engaged to Edwina Morton-West, and if some small voice deep within his soul ventured to hint that perhaps Miss Morton-West was not exactly the correct choice, all of his training as a gentleman was disciplined enough to suppress this thought into the darkest recesses.

Very shortly after Clare's encounter with the unfortunate Mr. Fox, he was able to conclude his project with the Foreign Office.

Lord Clarke winked at his protégé and clapped a fatherly hand upon his shoulder. "There's a satisfactory conclusion, my boy!" he said in his gruff manner. Dare say that this treaty at Ghent will drag for another month, and there's dashed little from Vienna these days. Suppose you'd like to go down to the country? Two sets of weddings in the offing, what?"

Clare, who was normally quite fond of his mentor, gritted his teeth. "Yes, sir," he said tonelessly.

"Don't scruple to tell you that we're all looking forward to meeting Thaddeus Clement's daughter when your mother decides to come into town again. Dare say she's waiting for your father to return to throw open Southcote House, what?"

"I dare say, sir." Clare replied mechanically, but he did pack his boxes that evening in preparation for the journey into Devon.

Miss Clement moved through her days oblivious of the rumors swirling about her in London. With a great deal of self-discipline, she endured the company of Edwina Morton-West and Lieutenant Steyland, whose none-too-subtle attempts at keeping an eye upon her doings, coupled with Miss Morton-West's frequent precepts on all matters of ettiquette, chafed sadly upon her already frayed nerves. In turn, Theodosia's vigilant chaperoning of her brother and Cynthia was winning her little regard from that corner. That they were closely involved in some secret scheme she was well aware. But if she had known the nature of that scheme, her anxiety would have been considerably lessened.

Cynthia's attempts at novel-writing were far above the average miss's, if only because of the dedication with which she applied herself to the task. And having a constant listener, ready to offer up his criticism of each installment, was definitely a source of encouragement to her. The tangled fortunes of Lady Caroline and company progressed apace, and if the work still bore traces of juvenilia, even so sternly honest an editor as Jefferson Clement had to admit that it showed definite promise.

Unfortunately, no author can completely surrender up a trace of ill will against an honest critic, no matter how clear or well-intentioned that person's suggestions for improvement in a work in progress. And Jefferson's rather academic mind, coupled with a youthful lack of tact, served rather effectively to depress the calf-love that had budded up between them, for Cynthia was sensitive to what she chose to see as the *integrity of her art,* and still unsure enough of herself to present a defensive front, even when she knew Jefferson's critiques to be perfectly accurate. It was not long before they fell into the habit of squabbling rather more like brother and sister than a pair of lovebirds, and while neither ceased to regard the other with affection, familiarity did suffice to breed a certain acceptance of their differences.

Lady Southcote, who believed that Cynthia was still rather too young to know her own heart and mind in marriage matters, was also wise enough to predict to herself that continued intimacy between Jefferson and Cynthia would produce just such a result. But, like Theodosia, she felt it best not to express her opinions, lest she cast the pair together in rebellious romance or cause her young house guest undue worry about the situation. Despite her daughter's predilection toward books and bluestocking attitudes, Lady Southcote reposed confidence that the girl's beauty would eventually serve to find her a suitable match, particularly now when so many young men were returning to civilian life following Waterloo.

In time, Miss Clement's common sense had asserted itself once again, and she was able to carry out her days without thinking upon Lord Claremont more than once or twice. She had to admit to herself that she missed his companionship, however, for there was no other gentleman with whom she could share as many of her interests. They all seemed to want to wrap her in cotton wool, as if she were something rather fragile and too delicate for the strenuous activities that she had enjoyed so much with Lord Claremont. He, at least, she reflected, did not object if she wished to gallop, or cast a fishing line, or practice target-shooting. Nor did he sulk if her skill at competitive sports was equal to his own, or protest if she happened to best him. So, she told herself, if her thoughts were upon him once or twice in the course of the day, it was because she missed his company. If Miss Morton-West made allusion to her plans as the future Lady Southcote, and Miss Clement found herself possessed of a most unladylike yearning to slap that complacent face, she was able to say that it was more due to what she considered to be presumption than to a most uncomfortable feeling of jealousy.

"Yes, I do think that when I should become Lady Southcote I shall cause that conservatory wing to be torn down and replaced with a rather more interesting Ruined Grotto, such as the one dear Lady Stavely has at Forbisham," Edwina said, smiling thinly and drawing on her gloves.

If Theodosia had not been so occupied with her own outrage, she might have noted the anguish that crossed

Lieutenant Steyland's gray face as he regarded Miss Morton-West, trailing her out to her curricle with doglike devotion.

Fortunately, this remark had not been uttered in Lady Southcote's presence, but not for the first time did that lady make her opinions of Miss Morton-West clear.

"Have they gone?" she demanded, thrusting her head into the salon, a pair of flower shears in her hand. "That female quite throws me into the dismals, Theo! She is so depressingly like her mother. . . . Honoria Steadly was always the most humorless female of my acquaintance—but I should say nothing!" she added as always, waving the shears in the air with the air of one who would prefer to be brutally martyred rather than speak ill of a female who had been her daggers-drawn nemesis for twenty years and more.

Theodosia, who had correctly begun to suspect that both ladies derived considerable satisfaction as well as entertainment from their hostility, merely nodded.

Lady Southcote fluttered a sheaf of papers in her hand. "The morning mail's just come in. Really, I do not know why Southcote should pay the postal receiving office a pound a year for early delivery when we never see the postboy until eleven o'clock! There's a note from Clare, a couple of invitations, and—oh, Theo! a note for you, with the marquess's seal upon it."

Theo's brows rose slightly as she took the paper from her hostess. For a few minutes, both ladies were quietly immersed in purusing their posts.

Scanning the marquess's long, scrawling fist, Theo saw nothing that would cause her to blush at first, and hastily scanned through the interesting news that Lady

Rumford had been delivered of a lusty son who was to be christened John Charles Vincent Michael Steyland-Younge in honor of both his grandfathers, that Durning was keeping a ruinously expensive opera-dancer in a very snug house on Half Moon Street, who could be seen daily in the park driving a team of matched whites behind a questionable *white-painted* phaeton, that young Fox had boxed the watch and been taken into custody again, so *foxed* that he had been foolish enough to give his own name at sessions-court, and that Countess Lieven and Princess Esterhazy had both been asking after her, and hoping that Lady Southcote would soon bring her up to London, and while he thought upon that gracious lady, would he be so kind as to present his most adoring compliments to her and to beg her expert opinion on the proper mulch for African palms to be pot-grown in his city conservatory?

It was only when Theodosia read his last scrawled sentence that she caught her lower lip between her teeth and frowned.

"Be assured, Peerless Theo, that my original offer still is open to you," she read.

"Yours and etcetera, Torville," she read aloud, shaking her head.

"Bad news, my love?" Lady Southcote asked with some concern.

Theo shook her head and smiled. "No. Lady Rumford has been brought to bed of a son, and Albert particularly asks that I present you with his *most adoring compliments,* and would you be so kind as to tell him the proper mulch for African palms in pots?" Her tone was so droll that Lady Southcote laughed, blushing quite prettily beneath her morning cap.

"I should certainly be glad to. Peat-bark, I think, and perhaps a very little Dover sand mixed with good sheep manure! Oh—Theo, here is a piece of news that might please you! Clare will be with us in a very few days! Lord Clarke has given him a week's leave. . . ."

Theo's expression was hardly one of overjoyed rapture. "I am sure that is very good, ma'am," she murmured, "And I am sure that Miss Morton-West will be very glad to hear it. If you will excuse me, I feel a headache coming on. . . ."

Theo picked up the skirts of her spring-muslin morning dress and swiftly walked out of the room, leaving Lady Southcote to stare after her with a most puzzled expression, since Theo was wont to experience the mildest aches and pains.

Owing to one thing and another, it was only a few days before Christmas when Lord Claremont finally arrived in Devon, his phaeton quite loaded down with the various packages that he meant to distribute among his family, friends, and servants. The day was cold and overcast in a manner that predicted the first snowfall of winter, and as he bounded out of his vehicle and up the shallow steps to the front door, his breath hung in frosty clouds before his face.

Despite the foreboding of his mood, he smiled at the holly wreath upon the knocker.

"Welcome home, sir!" Gibney exclaimed as he threw open the door.

Clare stepped into the hallway, drawing off his gloves. "Hullo, Gibney. Would you send one of the footmen out to fetch in that load of bundles before the twins see them?" he asked, allowing the retainer to divest him of his greatcoat and curly beaver hat.

"Certainly, my lord. . . ." He hurried out the doorway, where Sexton was already leading the team around to the stables.

"I'll have a cold nuncheon and a cup of tea sent round to the breakfast parlor, and I'll change my clothes. It's as cold as the devil's teeth out there! Is m'mother about?"

"Lady Southcote, Lady Cynthia, and Mr. Clement are on a shopping expedition in Honiton, my lord," Gibney informed him. "*Miss* Clement, however, is in the library, composing, I believe, letters," Gibney added hopefully. "If I may say so, Master Clare, the American lady has been a bit cast down of late."

Clare frowned. "She ought to be overjoyed, from what I hear," he muttered beneath his breath. Aloud he said, "Don't bother to announce me, Gibney. I'll have a look-in on Miss Clement as soon as I've changed away from my traveling dirt."

There was a setting of pine boughs and holly upon the mantel, and the fire was crackling on the hearth quite merrily, but Miss Clement was far from feeling the holiday spirit, as she sat chewing the nib of her pen, frowning down upon the sheet of paper before her. Beside her elbow, the blue baby-cover she had worked on in a very desultory manner for the past few weeks lay neatly folded, together with a congratulatory note to Lord and Lady Buxstead.

She had been engaged in trying to compose a suitable note to the marquess that would, with extreme tact, inform Dear Albert that while she would always regard him with the most affectionate terms of Friendship, she had decided that she would forever remain in the Maiden State, although she was . . .

Upon hearing the sound of Clare's wheels in the drive, she had jumped up from her chair and peered out the window. The sight of him was enough to cause her heart to thunder within her breast. Hastily, she withdrew from the window and sat down again in the chair, torn between hope and despair of her situation.

She had not long to wait.

"Ah, Miss Clement!" The cool tone Clare had meant to adopt died away when he beheld Theodosia in the flesh for the first time in many weeks.

As she rose from the writing desk to greet him he noted that she was a trifle paler than her usual color, and that there was the faintest trace of darkness beneath her large gray eyes. Despite these puzzling signs of stress, she looked very becoming in a merino morning dress of a delicate ivory, cut high to the throat and close-sleeved, ornamented at band and cuff with tiny ruffles of muslin, and gathered at the draped hemline in the very latest fashion with ivory silk ribands that exposed deeper ruffles beneath her skirts. Her russet curls were pulled away from her face in severe bands, but several recalcitrant curls had escaped their bondage to fall about her forehead.

With a stiff smile, so different from her usual manner, she moved forward to give him her hand. "Lord Claremont! How very good to see you. I'm afraid that I'm the only one here to greet you. Your mama and Lady Cynthia have gone over to Honiton and taken Jeff with them. Something to do with Boxing Day presents, I believe. You must be tired and chilled to the bone. Should you wish me to ring for some hot rum for you?"

Clare shook his head. "Oh, no! I have a nuncheon waiting for me in the breakfast parlor."

Theo nodded.

"Did I interrupt you? I perceive that you were writing letters."

"Oh, no," Theo shrugged with a show of indifference, "I—I just completed a letter to Lady Buxstead and was drafting a reply to Torville."

"Ah," said Clare shortly. He thrust his hands deep into the pockets of his biscuit-colored pantaloons, waiting for her to elaborate on her nuptial plans. When this information was not forthcoming, he shifted a bit uncomfortably and inquired, "And how *is* Torville?"

"From his letter, he goes on well enough. As full of plans as ever. He is redoing the conservatory of Torville house."

"I understand that I am to offer him my congratulations," Clare ventured, hoping this broad hint would elict, from Miss Clement's own lips, the news he had no real wish to hear. "Has the notice been fired off to the *Post* yet?"

Theodosia shook her head. "No, not yet—at least I have not seen it, but it is a wonderful thing, is it not? If it were I, I should be shouting it from the rooftops, but Debra—Lady Buxstead—is not in the best way of health quite yet, you see. But the event has caused a great deal of happiness among the Steylands, for they did despair of a happy outcome in the matter. There were, I believe, disappointments in the past." Theo worked the fringes of her shawl through her fingers, looking down at her feet.

Clare nodded. So, she was coming coy over the matter, was she? No doubt they had no wish to announce the engagement publicly until the treaty was signed and Thaddeaus Clement able to give his blessing to the match. With a twinge of hopelessness Clare realized that there was doubtless no opposition from that quarter. Clement, he understood, had raised his daughter to know her own mind in these matters, and Torville was, after all, an old and valued friend of the family.

With some effort, he managed a smile. "Well, I suppose you know your own mind, Miss Clement. But don't you think it wise to wait until you have communication from your father before you make any definite arrangements?"

Theodosia looked a little puzzled. "But I am only doing what is right, you know. I think that my father would expect me to handle this myself under any circumstances." She gave a little laugh. "After all, such things are really the province of females, you know, these rituals of life and family."

"I suppose you are right," Clare agreed uneasily. Clement must be a far more modern parent than he had envisioned. Perhaps these things were handled differently in America, after all. But dash it, must the girl act so coy about the matter? It was entirely unlike her. If *his* sister had snared a marquess, his mother would have been proclaiming it to the rooftops. But then again, Miss Clement did not have a mother to guide her.

"Excuse me, my lord," Gibney said at that moment,

appearing in the doorway. "Your repast is ready in the breakfast parlor."

"Ah," Clare said. "Have you eaten, Miss Clement? Would you care to join me?"

Theodosia shook her head. "Oh, no, I have had a cup of tea and a piece of fruit earlier. I shall finish this letter while I am still hot at hand with my words." She gave a little laugh which sounded strained and uncomfortable in her own ears. "I am not at all skilled with words, you know, and it takes me hours to compose the simplest statement."

"As you wish," Clare replied, imagining that she was no doubt composing a loverlike epistle and had no wish for his company when presented with what she must consider a far more pleasurable occupation.

At the doorway, a thought struck him and he turned once again toward her. "Ah, Miss Clement—"

She turned from the desk to look at him, feeling unwontedly hopeful.

"Perhaps you might like to go driving in the phaeton later? I think the snow shall hold off until this evening—ah, this time of the year is quite salubrious, if you do not mind the cold, for the countryside in its starkness has its own beauty."

Theodosia, for all of her noble intentions, was unable to resist the twin pleasures of Clare's company and a ride in his phaeton, even though she knew that this moment of pleasure would result in deeper pain later on. She smiled. "Oh, yes! I should like that above all things!" Sharply she recalled herself for such an unbecoming display of enthusiasm. "That is to say, yes, I think that would be greatly agreeable, Lord Claremont."

"Very well," Clare replied stiffly, and departed in search of a meal for which he had very little appetite, although he partook more liberally of the hot claret than was his normal wont.

It was just past three when Miss Clement descended the stairs, attired in a winter driving dress of nut-brown merino, cut rather dashingly close and trimmed elaborately round with bands of sable, closed from waist to throat with scribed brass buttons. Upon her russet curls she had placed a shallow-crowned driving hat of chocolate felt, banded with brass-colored braid and trimmed with three ostrich plumes which swept over one cheek. Over this she wore a dun-colored driving cloak lined with sable, and carried her muff of that fur over one arm. Neat half-boots of orange jean completed this ensemble, and as she approached Lord Claremont, she drew on a pair of Italian leather gloves.

Clare, who was not known to pay compliments to female attire, informed Miss Clement that that was a bang-up rig, and Miss Clement had to exert effort to keep surprise out of her tone as she thanked him for his compliment. Since his habit was covered by an ancient driving coat that spoke of many years' hard service, she did not feel compelled to return the compliment, but wondered to herself precisely why his lack of interest in his own attire was one of his more endearing habits. In any other gentleman, she thought, she would have found such negligence completely appalling.

When Clare threw Theo up into the perch, it was already growing darker. The weak gray sunlight cast long tree-shadows across the drive as they rolled away from the house, and the air which bit Miss Clement's face was distinctly sharp. Inside her muff, she rubbed her hands together.

For several miles, neither of them spoke. Miss Clement seemed lost in her admiration of the scenery, and Clare was occupied in the handling of this fresh team, which had not been taken out since he had departed for London some weeks previously.

They clipped along the back roads at a neat pace and passed through several quaint farm villages that Miss Clement had not seen before. For the first time since she had come to England, she gave herself over to admiration of the countryside and began to enjoy the brisk air and the sharp clarity of the day far more than she had expected to do.

About fifteen miles from Southcote Place, Clare reined in at a small Tudor Inn, suggesting that Miss Clement might like to refresh herself and have a glass of the hot cider for which the landlady of the Bird and Rose was locally famous.

Theodosia agreed to this scheme readily. "Cider! I have not had cider since—oh, years ago, when we still lived at home," she told Lord Claremont as he handed her down from the perch. "We used to make it from the apples in our own orchard, you see."

"Do you miss your home in America?" Clare asked with sympathy.

Theo nodded. "Sometimes. I should like to see it again. We left quite six years ago, and I have not seen it since. But it was one of the particular treats that my brother and I enjoyed in the fall, the fresh-milled cider from the orchard."

Mrs. Covey, a stout dame of indeterminate age and a great fondness for a gentleman she had known since his cradle days, bustled out of the inn to welcome them.

They were shown into the private parlor, where a cheerful fire burned in the grate and two comfortable chairs had been drawn up to the hearth.

"I know that Miss will not want to sit in the great, noisy common room," Mrs. Covey said firmly, "So, do you, Lord Claremont, just sit down, and I will send in Betsy with two tankards of my best mulled. It's been far too long since we've seen you here, my lord, and that's a fact." With a curtsey to Miss Clement, she bustled down the passageway.

Theo sank gratefully into one of the chairs and propped her feet on the grate, looking about the old oak-paneled room curiously. "This," she declared, "is what I always pictured England to be like. Why, this inn must be a hundred years old! And look at the carving in the wainscoting—flowers and leaves and trees— how very charming this place is!"

Clare stretched lazily in the other chair. "Actually, it's over three hundred years old. And quite one of the landmarks of our area. My father was used to bring my brother and myself here on our way to the seacoast, you see. I thought you might enjoy it."

Theo nodded, her reserve forgotten. "We have nothing so old in America. I dare say you would think it a very raw, untamed place, but it is not without a rugged beauty of its own."

In this manner, they contrived to converse about their homes and childhoods quite easily for some few hours. The mulled cider, brought in pewter tankards by a mob-capped young person who was clearly in awe of Miss Clement's American accent and grand clothes, was fragrantly spiced with cinnamon sticks and lemon peel.

It was rather a headier brew than Miss Clement had been used to at home, and not even the aromatic spices could disguise the sweet sharp bit of its potency.

"Very strong, but very good!" Miss Clement pronounced it. "Lord Claremont, you have excellent taste!"

Clare, who had been drinking Mrs. Covey's mull since he was a small boy, had no idea that a lady who could drink champagne all night might become a trifle giddy on an apple brew, and when Mrs. Covey bustled in with thick slices of her own homemade gingerbread, topped with that famous Devonshire clotted cream and still hot from her ovens, he immediately called for a second set of tankards.

Sicne his own judgment was slightly clouded from the quantity of claret he had consumed in place of his nuncheon, they managed to become quite gay together, and their mutual restraints seemed to have been thrown to the winds by the time that Clare noticed it was growing dark outside.

When they were mounted onto the phaeton again, they were both laughing over some jest they had contrived between themselves over the unfortunate Miss Ipstone's history.

"And after she was kidnapped by Barbary Pirates, of course, she managed to poison off the sultan and take his place upon the throne!" Theo crowed triumphantly as they bowled down the road.

They had come to the Honiton Pike, and the feeble orange sun was a ball above the bare trees when Clare handed Miss Clement the ribands and pointed to a cart-lane stretching off to their left.

"That's a shortcut to Lindsey Close," he said. "At this time of night it should be relatively free of traffic, if you should care to try your hand for a few miles. But keep 'em in close check, my friend, for they're a bit skittish still, and liable to run away if you aren't close-handed."

"Do but watch me, then!" Theo said recklessly as she seized the leather from Clare's hands and turned off the corner at a brisk pace.

For several miles, she held her leaders in check, driving in such a fine manner as made Clare praise his pupil rather too fulsomely than was his normal wont.

The darkening woods sped by, and they were fast approaching the village of Lindsey Close when a sharp and, for Theodosia, unexpected curve appeared ahead in the road, too late for her to pull her leaders into check.

The phaeton listed sharply to one side as she attempted to pull to her left, and Clare swiftly put his arms about her shoulders, seizing her wrists and pulling them back just in time to pull up the horses. The phaeton righted itself and the team pulled down to a trot, but it had been a narrow scrape that might have landed them in a damaging upset, and they were both a little shaken.

Clare brought his team to a halt, his arms still about Theodosia's shoulders. Beneath her furs, he could feel her body trembling.

Miss Clement turned her face toward Clare's, her expression woefully indicating that she expected a sharp set-down for such a piece of stupidity. But when she encountered that craggy face, looking into the deep-set green eyes so close to her own, she gave an involuntary gasp.

For one second that seemed as long as all eternity, Clare and Theo stared at one another, and the rest of the world seemed to fade away. Very slowly, his powerful arms tightened about her shoulders, and he brought his lips down upon hers in a crushingly rough kiss.

For only one second, she tensed in his embrace, poised between resistance and surrender. Then, with the tiniest of shrugs, she responded to him, her arms stealing out to wrap themselves about his strong shoulders, her hands caressing his dark hair.

Theodosia had been kissed before, but never quite like this. Nor, she discovered to her own surprise, had she ever enjoyed having her hat knocked away from her hair, or the sweet sensation of a man's rough skin against her own smooth cheeks. For one moment, she surrendered all other thoughts but the pleasure of such delightful closeness to Clare Southcote.

Too soon and too late he released her, shaking his head from side to side. "This is not right—" he murmured, moving away from her.

Theo nodded miserably, disguising her confusion in a search for her ridiculous hat, placing it back on her curls at a jaunty angle that belied her own *angst*. "No—no, it is not right at all!" she said in a low, tense voice, unable to meet his eyes.

Clare picked up the reins he had dropped. "I hope you will not—that is, Miss Clement—forgive me! I have behaved in a caddish manner!"

"Oh!" Theodosia murmured. "No—it was my fault entirely—so very *foolish* of me—the cider had gone to my head——" She broke off in confusion, looking down at her enormous sable muff as if it had suddenly become an object of enticing fascination.

Clare whipped up the ribands. "Let us think no more upon it," he said harshly. "Too much of Mrs. Covey's cider has made us both a trifle April-mad."

But for that April-madness, Theo thought unhappily, I should trade away my lifetime. Aloud she murmured assent in tones sturdier than her true feelings. "You are, of course, quite right, sir!"

The rest of the journey back to Southcote Place was accomplished in a miserable silence, each party in an agony over the imagined injured feelings of the other.

Nor, when the phaeton drew up in the stable yard, were they to be spared the attentions of other concerned persons. Sexton was first upon the scene, grasping the right leader's bridle, the first flakes of snow dotting his gray and grizzled head. "Where have ye been, Lord Claremont? There's been a rare to-do when you were not home by nightfall! My lady has been on tenterhooks to send us all out to look for ye. I expected to find you overturned in a ditch somewhere!" As he spoke, his eyes roved over the team and equipment for signs of damage.

"No need for such precautions and hysterics!" Clare said sharply as he jumped down from the perch and assisted Miss Clement to alight. "We merely tarried longer at the Rose than we intended. I had not seen Mrs. Covey in an age, you know, and——"

Without a word, Theo had picked up her skirts and darted into the house.

"Hang it!" Clare said, abruptly turning to follow her.

Sexton nodded sagely to himself and stroked his

beard. "Seems as if there be more trouble than trial there—here now, what are you standing there like a great booby for?" he abjured an overcurious stableboy. "Go you along and pull these cattle out of harness!"

Lady Southcote heard the side door open and close. "It must be them!" she said to Miss Morton-West, and darted into the hallway just as Gibney was emerging from belowstairs.

"Clare! Theo!" my lady said in agitated accents, rustling toward them in her merino half-dress. "Wherever have you been? I have been frantic with worry! Has some accident occurred to you? It is well past seven, and Alphonse is quite put out—dinner has been ruined—"

She turned Theodosia about, as if looking for signs of injury. Seeing Miss Morton-West standing in the doorway of the salon with a most unpleasant expression upon her long face, Theo gave a little gasp. "Oh, pray ma'am, I am sorry, but I do not feel precisely the thing—the cold—excuse me!" Without another word, she picked up her skirts and fled up the stairs, unable to contain the hot tears that had been threatening to spill down her cheeks for the past hour.

"Clare?" Lady Southcote asked in faltering accents.

With a great deal of effort, her son steeled his countenance. "It is nothing, ma'am. We merely stayed too long at Mrs. Covey's—you know that it has been ages since I last saw her, and then, on the way home in the twilight, I took a corner too close. Had to hold my team in close check for the better part of the drive from Lindsey Close."

Lady Southcote nodded, satisfied with this explanation, but Edwina gave a sniff. "And what, pray tell, were you and Miss Clement doing fifteen miles from home, Claremont?" she demanded in frigid accents. "And returning home after dark! Such behavior is *hardly* like you—though typical of Miss Clement!"

Clare's expression turned to stone and his eyes narrowed. "Will you permit me a word alone with Edwina, Mama? I am sure that Gibney wishes to speak to you about Alphonse's injured feelings, for he is standing in the belowstairs hallway making the most peculiar faces!"

Lady Southcote made a faint noise in the back of her throat as Clare stepped by her, gently impelling Edwina back into the salon and closing the door firmly behind him.

"Now, Edwina, perhaps we may talk more comfortably," Clare said in a voice which boded ill for anyone thus addressed.

Up until that moment, Clare had been careful not to display this side of his temper to Miss Morton-West, and she blinked at him, opening and closing her mouth several times before she could muster her composure.

Edwina's long face grew even longer, and she drew herself up to her full height. "Well, really, Claremont," she said in that tone which had always annoyed Guy when they were children, "What is one to think? You arrive at Southcote Place, without as much as sending word to me that you are home—and immediately go jauntering off over the countryside with that female, staying in strange inns and heaven only knows what!" Her upper lip began to tremble. "I can only wonder—really wonder, you know—exactly what is going on in your mind, Clare—have you run short of your senses that you are so constantly to be seen in Miss Clement's pocket? One would think you were as rakish as Guy!'

Clare's face grew even more forbidding. "And what of you, ma'am?" he demanded in a low voice, no less fraught with danger for its steel tones. "Every time I turn about, you—you are either at Southcote Place carrying tales of my family—or riding in that Navy fool's pocket, though what you should see in someone so obviously a *loose screw* is beyond me!"

"Loo—Claremont! Your language!" Miss Morton-West exclaimed in deeply shocked tones.

"Hang my language! Edwina, you have no right to cast aspersions upon Miss Clement! She is a guest in my mother's house. And pray tell me, Edwina! Is this the way you shall behave when we are married?"

"Well!" Miss Morton-West repeated coldly. "And I shall thank you not to call Lieutenant Steyland a name such as that! He is a most sensible and respectable gentleman, and from a well-connected family! The Steylands, I assure you, are of far older creation than the Southcotes! Peter—that is, Lieutenant Steyland!—is an admirable man, and certainly, his sentiments seem to be more in harmony with my own than yours, Claremont! He has been everything that is admirable, of so fine a tone of mind, and so genteel an outlook, that one could hardly be blamed for having every consideration for his friendship! If it were not for the Clements, I imagine he might have risen to his captaincy by now—" She tilted her head. "And besides, his mama and mine are old school friends!"

"Then perhaps you would find yourself better suited with this paragon of virtue than with such a rakehell as myself!" Clare snapped. "Oh, Edwina, do put aside these missish airs! They don't become you, playing the great Tragedy Jill!"

"Tragedy Jill!" Miss Morton-West sniffed. With trembling fingers, she withdrew the sapphire ring from her finger and almost threw it at Lord Claremont. But Miss Morton-West had not been brought up to throw things—even engagement rings—into gentlemen's faces, and she set it upon the table. "I think, Lord Claremont, that you and I would not suit, if this is what I should have to endure from you in our marriage!" Mustering her bombazine pelisse about her thin shoulders, she walked to the door, then turned, smiling at him in a very cold and evil-tempered manner. "Since you feel that Lieutenant Steyland and I should suit so well, perhaps I should tell you that he has pressed me to cry off from an alliance with so foul-tempered and —and *Corinthian* a person as yourself, for I should always be second to your sports—that horrid boxing!—and your odiously *boring* career!" With that she swept out of the room, calling for her curricle and her groom.

"Devil take it!" Clare said tersely. He picked up the ring and absently pushed it into his pocket, torn between a feeling that he had been played for a fool by Miss Morton-West and a vast, if unacknowledged, sense of release. For several minutes, he paced the floor of the salon, in the blackest abstraction, then opened the door to go in search of his mother.

What imp of perversion convinced him that he might find that lady in the library, when it was well-known that she rarely read more arduous literature than an engraved invitation, it was never to be known. But the scene that he encountered when he opened the doors to that chamber was more than enough to push his already sorely tried temperature to the boiling point.

By the light of a brace of candles, two golden heads were bent close together over a sheaf of papers on the desk; two shoulders touched, and two hands were almost entwined.

" ' "Oh, la!" proclaimed Lady Caroline airily, "I do not concern myself over such trifles as the marriage of a vicar's daughter, sir! Why, if I were to worry myself over those not of the *ton*, I dare say I should never have as much as a second to order myself a new gown! And do you not think this one is quite fetching—" ' " Lady Cynthia broke off her reading and looked up, frowning slightly into the darkness. "Clare! You have returned!" she exclaimed gratefully.

"My sister! Is Theo all right, sir?" Jefferson demanded, standing up.

"What have we here?" Clare demanded in tones of awful sarcasm. "Cynthia—I thought better of you! And under your mother's roof! Were you brought up no better than a crofter's daughter to act thus? And you—Mr. Clement! Taking advantage of an innocent female's inexperienced ways—and what, pray tell, is this?"

In a few strides he was across the room, snatching up the manuscript on the desk. Both Jefferson and Cynthia were pale in the flickering candlelight.

"Clare, pray—" whispered Cynthia in terrified tones.

"Lord Claremont, I must protest!" Jefferson added bravely.

Clare's angry eyes scanned the pages. "What, may I ask, is this, Cynthia?"

"A—a novel, Clare—please . . ."

173

"A novel," Clare repeated in that same sarcastic voice. "You are writing a *novel*, Cynthia? Good God, is this what comes of educating females? My own sister—writing a *novel!*" This last word was pronounced in such tones of contempt and loathing that Cynthia winced. "And pray, what do you plan to do with this piece of trash, sister?"

"I—I assure you sir, that Cynthia's novel is quite unexceptionable! There is nothing in its moral tone or its plot to put anyone to the blush! In fact, it's very much like real life—"

Courage, at least when faced with a very muscular gentleman of mature years in a state of white rage, was not one of Jefferson Clement's strong points. He broke off in confusion beneath Clare's awful stare, flushing up to the roots of his hair.

"*You*," Clare said in tones of contempt, "should be clapped in Devonshire Prison!"

"Clare!" Cynthia whispered, holding up her hands as if to fend off a blow.

"I shall deal with you later, miss! It is apparent that m'mother has allowed you too-free hands too long! You shall be packed off to your aunt Gunneston's in Bath as soon as possible! And pray that Father does not catch wind of this, if you think my temper hard, my girl!" Clare pointed to the door. "Go to your room, Cynthia! I am far too angry to deal with you now! If you were not out of the schoolroom, I should give you the spanking of your life!"

"Oh! You are a monster! A *monster*, Clare!" Cynthia, being one of those fortunate females who could look perfectly ravishing in tears, stared up at her brother from enormous blue eyes. "*Guy* would never have treated me so!" she flung over her shoulder as she ran from the room. "Guy may have been close to the wind, but he was never a *tyrant!* And besides, it is none of it what you think it is!"

This statement caused Clare to take a step toward Cynthia. Wisely, she retreated up the stairs, raining down an assortment of ancient schoolroom grievances upon her brother's head until the sound of her door slamming cut off her strident tones.

Clare returned his attention to Jefferson Clement, who was putting up his fists in a feeble effort to defend himself against possible attack.

"Cease this foolishness, lad!" Clare commanded in stentorian accents. "Try not to make yourself look to be a bigger cake than you are already! Do you think my sister is a housemaid to be kissed on the stairs?"

Jefferson warily lowered his fists and tried to summon up his dignity. "I assure you, sir, there has been nothing between Cynthia and I to put anyone to the blush! We—we have been working together on this novel of hers! I never so much as kissed her!"

Clare's powerful fists crushed the papers in his hand and he fixed Jefferson with a lowering gaze. "I would almost rather see you conduct a flirtation with Cyn than encourage her in these ridiculous notions of—of female equality and pretensions to literature! She is already too bookish by half, and it does not do for a young nodcock like you to be giving her ideas about having her drivel published! Only think how it would look—a miss barely into her second season publishing a novel! A novel! Trash for old widows and ape-leaders! Why, she's no more notion of literature than— than that set of parrots you foisted off on the schoolroom! Novels! Southcotes writing novels! A highly proper sort of female she should be, to be writing novels!" Clare shook his head angrily. "And you, you encouraging her! You ought to be horsewhipped!"

"You have no right, sir!" Jefferson replied hotly, his anger overcoming his lesser courage in defense of his friend. "No right at all to dictate to your sister! Perhaps if you read what she wrote, instead of condemning her out of hand, you might change your mind!"

"And it might be well if someone had dictated to *your* sister earlier on in her career! D'you think I wish to have a pair of Americans setting an example to my household? Southcote Place was a peaceable, well-ordered household before you two set foot in here!"

Jefferson gritted his teeth. "Name your weapons, sir!" He flashed. "I am certain that Torville will stand as my second!"

"Oh, take yourself off!" Clare replied impatiently. "What sort of a fool d'you think I am that I would call out a stripling schoolboy? The pair of you ought to be packed off to Devonshire Prison to cool your heels! Now, my boy, get out of my sight before I—well, just go!"

Jefferson mustered the remnants of his shattered dignity. "With pleasure, sir!" he said haughtily.

Alone in the library, Clare passed a hand over his hair and jerked impatiently at his cravat. "Devil take it!" he muttered again.

Lady Southcote appeared in the doorway shortly thereafter. She peered anxiously into the room and saw her son, seated carelessly in a wing chair before the fire, reading a bulky manuscript, with a slight, sardonic twist to his mouth.

Such *contretemps* as she had overheard had not passed in the household since the eldest children had moved out of the schoolroom, and her first impulse was to demand of her son what he had said to cause everyone to retire to their various chambers in such disorder.

Being a rather nervous female, and as much in abhorrence of Unpleasantness as Clare seemed to thrive upon it at times, she regarded her son's glowering face for a second or two, then wisely decided to retire to the soothing ministrations of her abigail, who knew exactly how to soothe her mistress's agitated headaches when Clare was in One of His Moods.

Had she but known the misapprehensions under which her son labored, the course of events might have turned out in a far more peaceful fashion.

CHAPTER NINE

In a state of considerable agitation, Cynthia found Theodosia in her room, her eyes dry, but suspiciously red-rimmed, an embroidered dressing gown wrapped about her nightdress.

"Theo!" that damsel whispered, throwing herself rather dramatically upon a chair. "All is lost! Oh, he is the most odious brother in the world! I know that it is not kind to say it—indeed, it is excessively shocking! —but I could almost wish that it were Clare instead of Guy who had fallen in Spain?"

Pulling herself together with some effort, Theo found a handkerchief and, piece by piece, solicited the rather garbled reenactment of the scene in the library from her young friend. While Cynthia's descriptions were tinged with the melodrama so beloved of novelists, Theodosia's mood was not such that she could readily perceive the difference between fact and fantasy, and she was already considerably agitated when Jefferson stumbled into the room, his face as pale as his cravat.

"Devonshire Prison!" he gasped, and these fatal words caused his sister's heart to thunder in her chest. "He means to pack us off to Devonshire Prison, Theo!"

"And I am to go to my aunt Gunneston's in Bath!"

Cynthia declaimed in tragic accents. "Which is probably as bad!"

Theodosia fairly threw herself upon her brother. Her hands dug into his shoulders, and she peered anxiously into his face. "He did not say that!" she pleaded, but Jefferson nodded miserably. "He says that the pair of us are to be packed off to Devonshire Prison!" Jefferson shook his head. "I don't mind so much for myself—but for you, Theo—"

She pressed her hands against her cheeks, shaking her head, her eyes wide and hollow. "He could not—oh, he would not! Oh, no! And it is all my fault! No doubt our dear friends Miss Morton-West and Lieutenant Steyland have had a hand in this, but oh, if I had not—" Her voice trailed off, and she wrapped her arms about herself, pacing the room.

Jefferson and Cynthia both watched her hopefully. "Can you think of something Theo?" her brother asked.

She pulled her hands through her hair. "Oh, if I had not—but he is—he will—he is the foulest beast in nature! If I were a man—but that does not bear thinking about! There must be another solution—Lady Southcote—no—Lord Southcote, of course, but he is in Ghent, and it will take weeks to send a letter—by that time, we might both be dead of prison fever. We could go, of course, and allow him to—but that will not do, for what I know of prisons is very little, but I understand that they are foul places, full of rats and Lord only knows what—" She continued to pace the room, biting her lower lip.

"Theo always thinks out loud when she is in a tangle," Jefferson told Cynthia. "But depend upon it, she'll think of something. She always does," he added with such complete faith in his sister that she was cast into even greater agonies lest she betray his innocent trust.

She continued in this fashion for several minutes, chewing upon a strand of her hair, while the two young persons watched her curiously.

"The marquess!" Theo said at last. "Oh, Jeff! I have it! Albert!" She threw her arms about her brother and hugged him soundly. "Should you very much mind if I were to marry Albert?"

"Dash, Theo, this isn't a time to be thinking about getting hitched up, and to Albert Steyland at that!" Jeff said doubtfully.

Theo shook her head. "No, no, you see, Albert has offered for me, Jeff! If I were to marry him, then there would not be anything Lord Claremont could do us, for we should be under the protection of the Marquess of Torville! And he's a member of Parliament, I think, so he must have some power to protect us! And he's as rich as pudding pie, so if he can't do anything directly, I'm sure he can buy us something!"

"He has a seat in the House of Lords," Cynthia said doubtfully. "But I don't think he's ever taken it. Torville in the House?"

"Besides, Theo, that won't crack it," Jefferson added gloomily. "He's in London and we're here."

"Then we shall go to London!" Theo said firmly. "Although I am not quite certain how we may accomplish that, or even precisely in which direction London lies. Although I am sure that Cynthia must know...." She looked inquiringly at the girl.

"If one does not have one's own carriage, one may

180

hire a post chaise, from Honiton." Cynthia frowned. "But that is rather expensive."

"And we have not five dollars between us, and only a few hundred lira. Not a pound note or a shilling!" Theodosia sat down upon the edge of her bed and rested her head against her hand. "I would sell my mother's emeralds, if I could find a respectable jeweler in Honiton—but then, you may be sure that it would get back to Lady Southcote, and she must not become entangled in the scheme, and even if we could hire a post chaise, everyone would recognize us—our accents stand out like sore thumbs—and you may rest assured there would be a great hue and cry raised and *he* would come after us!"

"Oh, it is true!" Cynthia said bitterly. She thought for a moment. "I have twenty pounds until quarter-day, when I shall get my allowance. If you were to take the London Mail, you might contrive!"

"No, that wouldn't do either," Theo said, tapping one finger against her cheek. "For we should still arouse suspicion."

"Also, it is excessively uncomfortable, I believe," Cynthia said doubtfully. "One of our maids goes to visit her sister in London, and she is obliged to have a cheap seat outside, and she says that it is excessively wretched to be exposed to the weathers. And the highwaymen!" she added.

"That doesn't bother us!" Jefferson said stoutly. "We were used to taking the coach between Philadelphia and Washington when father was in the Senate. We contrived."

"If you would lend us your twenty pounds, Cynthia, I am certain that I would be able to pay you back as soon as I am safely married to—to Albert! I think I may have found a way to contrive, after all." With a look upon her face which Jefferson knew only too well, Theo bolted from the bed and pulled a portmanteau from her wardrobe.

"Whatever it is, Theo, I don't like it," Jefferson said warily.

"Stuff and nonsense!" Theo said over her shoulder. "Everyone will be looking for a young man and a female in the first stare of fashion, but I doubt very much if a young buck and his valet in a phaeton will cause much comment. Thank God I am tall, Jeff, for I do believe that snuff-brown coat of yours and those buckskins will fit me quite tolerably. But under no circumstances will I wear that dreadful waistcoat of yours embroidered round with cherry-stripes!"

"Theo!" Jefferson hissed in awful tones.

"Now, Cynthia, if you would be so good as to fetch down your twenty pounds, I think that Jefferson and I might contrive to hitch Lord Claremont's phaeton and team without waking Sexton—thank God the grooms sleep in the servants' quarters, or there might be the devil to pay. And I think also I might wish to borrow that very nice set of dueling pistols of Lord Claremont's—"

"Theo!' Jefferson repeated.

Lady Cynthia Southcote, lost in admiration for the courage of her American friend, said nothing, only gazed upon her with adoring eyes.

"I think I can handle the team well enough to get us to the next posting-house. And from there, we may take the stage to London. D'you think I can contrive a reasonably good Oxonian accent?" She giggled, caught up in the threads of high adventure. "Oh, Jefferson, don't look at me with daggers drawn! We shall leave Lord Claremont's phaeton and team there, and he may retrieve them at his leisure. And I am sure that Albert will recompense him for any damage done."

"Won't Clare be furious?" Cynthia laughed. "He prizes those grays above anything else!"

"He knows they shall come to no damage at my hands," Theo said calmly. "What I shall do is tell the innkeeper that—that I have shot my blunt at the races—Newmarket? And that I am forced to take the stage into London, and that my brother will come along for the team within a day's length. Cynthia, you must wait until you are certain we are in safe in London before you tell your brother anything! Do not let him bully you! If you appear to be as much at a loss as the rest of the household, I am certain that he will not question you too closely."

"I can do that," Cynthia promised, a martial light in her eyes. "For your sakes!"

"This is grand indeed!" Theo said. "I have not had such an adventure since that time we were in the Alps—"

"Please, Theo, don't remind me," Jefferson pleaded. "Every time I think about that bandit, I get ill again—"

"Oh, never mind that," Theo said impatiently. She opened the portmanteau and dug about in its contents for a few seconds before she emerged with a pair of sewing shears. Standing in front of the mirror, she began to hack ruthlessly at her long curls. "I think I shall make an admirable gentleman, don't you?" she asked her astounded audience.

It was just past the dawn hour when a high-perch phaeton, drawn by a team of exhausted grays, drew up in the yard of the Bird in Hand on the outskirts of Salisbury, and two young gentlemen descended from the high perch.

The taller of the two stamped his cold feet against the snow-covered cobbles, muttering at his companion. His golden locks were concealed beneath a low-crowned beaver hat of somewhat antiquated mode, and a heavy red muffler was wrapped about his face. Over his clothes he wore a gray greatcoat that reached down to his ankles, from the shoulders of which he brushed away a tracery of snow.

The slighter gentleman, who had been handling the reins, removed his felt hat to knock away the white powder and readjusted the voluminous folds of his drab cloak, looking about the courtyard curiously.

"No, let me do the talking, Jefferson, you never were any good at play-acting," Theodosia Clement adjured her brother.

"I still think this is a bad idea, Theo," Jefferson replied in a low voice. "He could be after us at any moment."

Theo, fond a sister as she was, had begun to feel a definite sense of annoyance with her brother. Their long and exhausting ride over rough and strange roads with a feisty team unused to the driver had not been an easy one for her. She was tired, and a bit afraid despite the brace of pistols in her belt, borrowed from Mr. Southcote's gun room, and very thirsty and hungry besides.

"Oh, Lord, Jeff, he won't be awake for hours yet, and when he is, we'll be on our way to London on the stage." She walked to the door of the inn, and after one glance over his shoulder at the empty road, Jefferson followed her.

"I'd still like to stop and see Stonehenge, as long as we're here," he was saying as he followed her through the passageway. Theo gave him a sharp elbow in the ribs, for the landlord, still yawning, was just emerging from the taproom, looking at them curiously.

Theodosia had thought her disguise to be rather clever until it fell under that good man's shrewd and suspicious gaze. Having been, like his father before him, and his father before that, in the hostelry business all of his life, he had learned to size up his customers at a glance, and what he saw of Theo and Jefferson did not impress him. It was clear that they were not Quality-make, nor anything like. In fact, he thought, taking in Theo's slight figure and smooth face, they looked like a pair of runaway 'prentices, and up to no good.

"Excuse me, sir," she said in her best imitation of her hosts' accents, "but what time is the next stage for London? And can you take charge of my phaeton and team until my brother comes to fetch it away?"

The landlord wiped his hands on his apron, and glanced out the window. He needed only one glance at Lord Claremont's exquisite phaeton and team to know that these two were not runaway apprentices, as he had first thought. The beetle-browed face he turned upon the Clements was far more suspicous than before.

Theo jingled the guineas in her pocket suggestively. "Dropped a great bundle at the races, don't you know," she said, hoping her voice sounded properly masculine and Oxonian. "Forced to take the stage back to town. But m'brother'll be along shortly, and he'll pick up the team. And stand the blunt," she added.

To the landlord, the pair looked hardly old enough for university, but mentally he calculated the gratitude of a wealthy parent who would retrieve both sons and phaeton, and smiled upon them jovially.

"Well, now, that's a different matter. Young gentlemen will have their ups and downs, I always tell my missus, and many's the lad we've had in here forced back by the mail to Town! Would you care to step into the common room, then, and I'll hist up the maid to bring ye a spot of breakfast? The London Mail will be through here at a leetle past eight, as you can see by the schedule posted by the door." He went to summon the ostlers.

Theodosia sighed gratefully. "Yes, breakfast," she said.

While she and Jefferson ravenously devoured several slices of ham, a great dish of eggs and kidneys, and the larger part of a blueberry-preserve tart, they watched as the inn filled up with passengers for the Mail. There was a fat woman and her daughter, each one with a basket of live chickens, who quarreled bitterly and loudly between themselves, a thin parson who drank weak tea as he perused his gospels, and a pair of countryfolk who were obviously on the first stage of their honeymoon, who sat in the corner by the chimney, staring into one another's eyes as if nothing else in this world mattered.

The sight of this last couple gave Theodosia a slight twinge, but with food inside of her and a warm fire by which to warm her hands, she soon felt better.

"We shall be at the marquess's in a very few hours, then all will be well!" she promised Jefferson, who yawned and looked gloomy.

At a little past eight, the lumbering Mail drew up in the yard, and the coachman, a large, very important looking man in a spotted kerchief and the bright red coat which proclaimed his profession, entered the common room. "All 'board for the London Mail!" he announced, regally accepting the glass of heavy wet the barmaid hastened to draw for him. "Outside passage only! We're as full as we can hold, for the snows from the north have delayed the Midland Flyer."

At this pronouncement, the mother and daughter put up a great fuss, insisting that their tickets procured inside seating for them as far as the metropolis.

The parson joined into this argument, calling upon various scriptures to support his claim, and Theodosia was able to purchase tickets for the outrider without attracting undue attention. But when she returned to Jefferson, she looked a little distraught. "Fifteen pounds for the pair of us and two portmanteaus! Shocking! But I dare say we shall contrive, for he did not want to take us at all."

"But I dare say you contrived, Theo," Jefferson yawned. "Let us board before I fall asleep! I think I shall doze all the way into town."

Theo patted his arm reassuringly, and they went out to board the cumbersome vehicle. The snow was falling rather more swiftly now, and the outrider suggested dubiously that it was liable to get worse afore it got better.

" 'Board the London Mail!" the coachman cried as

the quarreling ladies climbed up beside the Clements, still clutching their baskets of fowl.

The big man climbed into the box and Theo suppressed a yawn, leaning against Jefferson. "Soon," she whispered.

With a single blast of the coachman's horn, the big stage rolled out of the courtyard and down the road.

Just at that moment, the landlord appeared around the corner of the building, together with an officious-looking man in sober black clothes which proclaimed his profession to be that of magistrate.

"Them's the ones!" the landlord puffed, out of breath. "Runaways! You mark me!"

"Listen! Slow that coach! King's law!" The magistrate cried, but the coach was already far down the road.

Oblivious of their narrow escape, the Clements gave themselves over to their journey. Used to hard traveling, they did not complain, as did the stout mother and daughter, of the pelting snow that stung their faces, nor, like the sour parson, of the ceaseless bump and jostle of the badly sprung vehicle. They were not far down the road before Theo begun to wish that she had her sables, and Jefferson turned his muffler twice more about his face. They huddled together for warmth, drowsily watching the white-covered countryside pass them by, half hearing the desultory conversation of the coachman and their fellow passengers as no more than a vague and unpleasant buzzing.

Fortunately their fellow travelers were all far too engrossed in their own discomfort to pay much note to two sleepy boys, and both Jefferson and Theo were able to doze off for brief stretches of time.

Theo's slumber was haunted by vague, gruesome nightmares in which the outrider's yard of tin heralded the overtaking of the mail by Lord Claremont, who shouted the dreaded words *Devonshire Prison!* into her ears. And she would awaken with a start to brush the snow away from her face and look upon Jefferson, who slumbered beside her, oblivious in his faith in his sister and her ability to handle and disentangle them both from any emergency situation which might arise.

With a small sigh, Theo would bury herself deeper into her woolen cloak, trying hard not to allow her mind to cast too deeply upon Lord Claremont Southcote, or upon the fate which awaited her in London. Of course, she thought, she would try her best to make Albert a very good wife; her feelings toward Lord Claremont were, she reminded herself furiously, addlepated. How could she possibly cherish the tenderest emotions toward a man who had threatened her with prison? It made no sense at all. . . . She pressed her fingers to her temples and resolutely put her unhappy thoughts out of her head.

In the normal course of events, Theo would have hugely enjoyed the sights and sounds which attended the arrival of the Mail at the Pelican in London, and would have been instantly curious to take in all aspects of this part of the metropolis. The Clements had once been in this city many years ago, and she hoped to salvage enough from memory to have some vague sense of how they might go about.

But it was well past nightfall when they were set

down in the yard of this immense depot, and Jefferson proclaimed himself frozen through and impatient to seek out the marquess's hospitality. All he wanted, he said sleepily, was a warm bed and a hot toddy to set him aright. Since he punctuated this remark with a large sneeze, his sister's anxiety was greatly increased.

Not without some difficulty did Theodosia finally obtain the services of an ancient hackney coach, for the competition for one of these vehicles was fierce, and she was several times rebuffed by drivers who saw the chance of a better fare in persons who appeared to be in better circumstances than herself.

Eventually, however, they were taken up by a driver with a bone-spavined nag, and settled themselves in the redolent cabin of what must have been, some forty years previous, a gentleman's curricle, now in such a sad state of depletion that the stuffing was emerging from the squabs.

They were no sooner settled into this grim conveyance than the hack's long face appeared through the trap demanding their direction, and Theo was forced to dig in her pockets for the marquess's address.

"Hist up now, I h'ain't got all night," the hackney snapped as Theo unfolded the sadly crushed epistle and sought to make out the address by the dim illumination of the new gaslights outside the window.

"Number fourteen Grosvenor Square!" Theo finally said imperiously, stung by this man's rudeness. "And be quick about it, my good man!"

The hackney's only reply was a sardonic laugh and the slamming of the trap. But they were soon moving through the streets, and she began to feel her spirits slightly restored.

"We'll be all right and tight soon," she promised Jefferson, patting his hand.

"I hope so," he murmured, his head thrown back against the dirty squabs. His face was pale, accented by two bright flames of color in his cheeks, and his breath was coming in wheezing gasps. Alarmed, Theo put a hand to his forehead.

"You're burning up, Jeff!" She said in alarm. "Do you feel all right?"

"Oh—yes, fine!" Jefferson replied bravely, although his head was spinning and, dispite the cold, he had an urge to remove as much of his clothing as he could. He sneezed again, and his sister handed him a handkerchief, assuring him that Albert would see that he had a hot bed and a good doctor.

After what seemed to be an eternity, the ancient hackney rolled to a stop, and Theo peered out the window to see a row of imposing mansions.

The rap slid open again and the leering face of the hack peered down at them. "Here we are, lads, fourteen Grosvenor Square, although it appears that no one's awake." This information seemed to give him pleasure. With one glance at the darkened windows of the house, Theodosia could confirm the truth of his statement. But she was undaunted, and began to gather their portmanteaus. "That'll be two quid," the hack said quickly.

Theo, thinking of her depleted purse, was about to protest, but Jefferson sneezed again, and she handed over the fare without question, helping her brother to ascend from the vehicle.

The hackney, amazed at the ease with which he had nobbled two country bumpkins, swiftly gee'd up his horse and rolled off down the street before they could have time to reconsider the high tariff.

"Theo, it doesn't look as if anyone's at home," Jefferson said uneasily, looking up at the darkened windows, shivering slightly.

"Nonsense!" his sister said firmly, and mounted the steps. She gave the knocker a sharp rap, and listened to it echoing through the hallway on the other side of the black door. The lion's head seemed to stare at her in a mocking way, and she rapped again.

Jefferson, his strength gone, leaned against the post and coughed. Theo gave his muffler another wrap about his throat, and desperately pounded against the door with her fists.

Eventually, from within, there came the sound of shuffling footsteps, and the great front door was opened a crack. An individual whose vest, hastily thrown over his nightdress, proclaimed him to be a footman, peered out the opening with a jaundiced eye. "What d'ye mean, rousin' a gentleman's house at this hour of the night?" this individual demanded, upon ascertaining that the two persons upon the doorstep were, to judge by their raiment, of no consequence whatever to the Marquess of Torville.

"Will you please rouse up the Marquess," Theo said, all pretense of anything but her own American accent gone, "and tell him that Miss Clement desires him immediately?"

The footman fixed an eye upon this intruder. "And 'oo might you be?" he demanded, not unreasonably, "to be asking for my lord in Miss Clement's name?" For the reputation of the American Lady had not escaped the marquess's servants.

"I," Theodosia said, "am Miss Clement."

If she had expected this pronouncement to gain her entry into the sacred portals, she was disappointed, for this guardian only snorted with contempt. "And I'm the bloody Queen of Sheba, lad! Be off with you afore I call out the watch! Go home and sleep it off!"

With these words, the door was slammed in Miss Clement's face. "But I am Miss Clement!" She protested to the wood.

"Be off, or I'll throw you down the steps!" the doughty footman called over his back, retreating up the stairs to his bed with several adjurations upon the follies of young men.

Theodosia Clement raised both hands to pound again upon the door, but her brother protested.

"Don't, please, Theo! The last thing we need is to cause a commotion and attract attention! Then even the marquess couldn't rescue us! We're the enemy!"

Theodosia's common sense got the better of her temper, particularly when she saw a passerby, lantern in hand, standing at the corner of the street, regarding them in a most suspicious manner. "Oh, Lord, we are in duck's soup, Jeff," she murmured beneath her breath. Quickly, she slipped an arm beneath his shoulders and supported him away down the street in the opposite direction, their portmanteaus quite forgotten on the marquess's doorstep.

"Drunken lads, out on a lark," the passerby said to himself, looking at his watch. What was none of his business was none of his business, for he had been young once also. But he did wonder at the incident.

Despondent, cold, and tired, Theodosia and Jefferson walked down the quiet white street with no direction in mind. In that part of town there were no ordinaries, no taverns that might have offered them a hot beverage and a place to regroup their thoughts. Only row upon row of august mansions seemed to line the streets, and they stumbled on.

"If we can but find shelter for the evening, in the morning I shall think of something," Theodosia said with more confidence than she was feeling. It had not occurred to her that the marquess's privacy would be zealously guarded by an army of servants. Where a finely dressed Miss Clement, accompanied by her brother and a host of baggage, might have been a trifle unusual upon Torville's doorstep, it would still have gained her instant admittance. But two rather travel-stained and shabbily dressed young men could not even gain entry through the servant's hall. This was a new problem for Theodosia, who had always been used to a reception befitting her consequence, and one that she understood would take considerable thought to resolve.

But she adjured her brother to buck up, and to but walk a few blocks more, in search of a public house open at that hour of the evening.

Although their wandering brought them into a part of town that was considerably less elegant than the neighborhood in which the marquess made his dwelling, they were still unable to discover an ordinary catering to trade at three in the morning.

At last they drew abreast of a small stone chapel set between a draper's shop and a livery stable, and Jefferson, seized with a fit of coughing, leaned against the wall.

"Rest for the body—peace for the Soul," Theo read from the sign above the door. "Well, in the ordinary way of things, it is not precisely what I would wish, but beggars cannot be choosers." She took Jefferson's hand. "At least it will be a place to sit, if the doors be unlocked, and it will be out of the snow. *And,*" she added with a flash of humor, "if they come for us, we can claim sanctuary."

"Anything!" Jefferson wheezed.

The small chapel was obviously of some nonconformist sect, for even in the cold darkness Theo could see that it lacked the rich appointments of the churches she had been used to seeing, and the mottoes hung upon the peeling plaster walls seemed more concerned with hellfire and brimstone than the gentler messages of the New Testament. But there were some rather cold, hard-looking benches to sit upon, and though it smelled of must and old hymn books and mice, it was a few degrees warmer than the street outside.

"I suppose we may stay for an hour or two and pray that the sexton doesn't discover us. If anyone comes in, we must at least look as if we are praying," Theo said, settling herself on the pew with a small, slight sigh of relief. She wriggled her frostbitten toes in her boots, wishing she had thought to pull on a pair of strong woolen stockings when she had adopted her disguise.

Jefferson, looking extremely miserable, merely sneezed again.

"God bless!"

The third voice seemed to echo through the hollow space, and Theo's hand went to the pistol at her belt.

CHAPTER TEN

"Well, by God, Sexton, harness m'father's curricle! There's not a moment to lose!" Clare shouted over his shoulder, turning back to his extremely agitated mama. "Now, ma'am—" he began, but she held up the note in her hand.

"Devonshire Prison! Clare, how could you have threatened those children with Devonshire Prison? Oh, when I think about the pair of them out on the highways, with no more sense of how to go on than—than Gussie and Hester, I am quite prostrate! Is there nothing you can do?"

"Only seek to follow them!" Clare replied grimly. "How was I to know the boy would take me seriously? Well you know that Nurse Finch used to threaten Guy and me with Devonshire Prison—it was a child's bogie, something to frighten us into our best behavior. Good God, Mama, if I were not so afraid for Miss Clement's safety, I would wring her neck! Cynthia, be quiet, do! What crack-brained notion did you take into your head to allow them to go off like that? Had you no idea what could happen if they run afoul of the law? With twenty pounds between them and a stolen phaeton! Good God, Cynthia, do stop that wailing."

That lady, whose courage had rapidly broken

beneath the grim pictures painted of the possible fates of the Clements by her brother, only turned her handkerchief in her hand and sniffled even louder. "It was quite your fault, Clare!" she said vehemently. "Coming the monster upon Jeff, and treating Theo as if—as if she were a schoolroom miss, and then threatening them with Devonshire Prison."

"And all because you broke off with Edwina, which, Clare, I do not scruple to tell you, now that the business is finished, was one of the most fortunate pieces of luck that has ever occurred in this family! Edwina has always been the most detestably odious child, exactly like her mother—I, for one, shall be glad not to have to exchange more than common civility with Honoria Morton-West again! What possessed you to offer for her in the first place—a worse misalliance I could not hope to find!" Lady Southcote said firmly.

"Then perhaps you find the engagement between Miss Clement and Torville more to your liking, ma'am, since it must have been promoted under your consent!"

Lady Southcote blinked. "Engagement? Between Torville and Theodosia? Certainly his attentions to her were always most particular, but I have not heard her say that she entertained thoughts of returning his affections, until I found this note."

"She's only marrying him," Cynthia sniffed, "because you miffed her, and she has nowhere else to go! They were never engaged! Clare, how could you be such a cake?"

This piece of news gave Clare pause. "But all of London is saying—" He grasped his mother by her shoulders, peering earnestly into her face. "Ma'am, is what you say true? Theo—Miss Clement was never engaged, not even secretly, to Torville?"

Her ladyship shook her head. "Of course not, Clare! Although he was most particular in pressing his suit, I do not think her affections were strong—"

Clare clasped his mama to his chest in a crushing embrace, then kissed his sister. "This is a famous piece of news! Could it be possible—but no! Yes! I must not waste a moment! If I am but in London in time, then I wish I may see her steal a hundred—no, a thousand phaetons from me! Mama, should you object terribly to a connection between ourselves and the—but I must go! She has five hours upon me, but even Torville will need time to procure a special licence—only pray that they have not gone to Gretna!" With these mysterious utterances, Clare was out the door, leaving his astounded mother and sister to stare after him.

"Has he gone completely mad?" Cynthia demanded through her sniffles. "I always knew he would, with that temper of his—"

But Lady Southcote merely smiled fondly at her son's form as he hopped into the curricle and whipped up the horses, "No, my dear, I think, for the first time since Guy's death, he has found his senses again!" She pressed her hand against her bosom. "I, too, pray that he may not be too late," she murmured.

" 'Ere now, no need for a fire-rod," said the creature who was approaching Theodosia and Jefferson. "It should be as plain as the clappers on your phiz that I ain't a-going to harm you, nowheres near."

In the dim light, Theodosia made out the form of a female arising from one of the rear pews. She was no older than Miss Clement, but to go by the tawdry splendor of her toilette, the female was certainly not a lady. Upon her crimped and henna'd hair, she wore a jockey bonnet of bronze velvet, ornamented with several bunches of cherries and flowers, together with two ostrich plumes of brightest purple, all of this held together with an amazing profusion of ribands. She might have been pretty, had her expression been a little less hard, and her features not so heavily painted with rouge and kohl. Theodosia thought that a French pelisse of royal purple, trimmed with strips of ancient and moth-eaten ermine, over a tangerine spangled dress of almost transparent muslin, did little to add to her appearance. But the smile upon the woman's face was genuine enough, and her brown eyes may have been shrewd, but they held little guile. "I moves under the label of Riband Peg"—she touched the collection of bands on her bonnet and smiled—"and I'm in the diving lay. You look like a couple o' flash coves, you do. Your lay be hen-and chicken?"

Fortunately, most of this speech was incomprehensible to the Clements, both from Riband Peg's strong East End accent and her use of wholly alien cant terms. But Theo understood enough of her new acquaintance's introduction to understand that her occupation was not what Theo had originally surmised it to be.

"I'm not quite sure what my *lay* is," Theo replied, "But I think that I do not have one. And neither does my brother."

Riband Peg drew closer to them, looking into Theo's face, then down at her figure. "You ain't no cove—you're a mort!" She said, nodding her head several times in a most self-satisfied manner. "I can mostly always pick out a moll—and a jill, also, for that matter. A way o' bein' a talent you gets in my profession, for when you wants to go dippin' pockets, you got to learn these things."

From this interesting statement, Theodosia discovered that Riband Peg's occupation was picking pockets, and she nodded understandingly. "Well, then, my brother and I do not have a lay at all. But my name is Theodosia Clement and this is my brother, Jefferson Clement."

Jefferson sneezed and nodded at Miss Peg in an awed manner. It was clear that he had never seen such a person in his entire career. For her part, Riband Peg looked at him closely, clucking her tongue. "You look like the fish what's eaten the cork, me lad. That's a fine great head you've got upon ye." From a pocket inside the lining of her pelisse, she produced a relatively clean linen handkerchief. "See 'at? Got strawberry leaves upon it. I dipped it from a swell out in kens wi 'is flash cronies, passed out on blue ruin. If I'd known it were a duke, I'da dipped his ticker, I woulda. 'Is watch, to you folks. Handkerchief like that, maybe Long Sally 'll gimme a shilling. A ticker, now there I could glom me a coachwheel, and be off me lay for a week, just a washin' up and eatin' oranges. I do love oranges, when I can get 'em."

"Thank you," Jefferson said, blowing his nose rather loudly. "I wish you could have—uh—dipped a couple more, for my nose is running very badly."

Riband Peg frowned and rolled her hands up into little fists, which she dug into her waist. One worn and sodden merino boot tapped on the bare wooden floor.

"I thought you two was a trifle rum. There ain't many as knows this 'ere place to be an easy ken on a cold night when the pickin's is slim. Blow me to 'ell if I can place that accent, but it sure ain't from London—or England, for that matter!"

Theo's hand went to her belt again, but Riband Peg merely shrugged and sat down on the pew. "You ought not to be so 'asty to be pullin' that popper, Theodosia—if that's your true label. What you's doin' ain't my drub, if you catch my meanin', for diver I may be, but I'm an honest mort for all o' that, and got no truckle wi' the law, no more'n' you, I think! But iffen I were to be you, I'd want to get that brother o' mine into some place warmer nor this mission, afore the blue-runs does take 'im off, a-like they did me little sister three winters ago. And she started out the same—a hanking an' cuttin' a sniff, and next ye knew, we was a laying her out." Riband Peg nodded wisely at Theo, who was watching Jefferson with some alarm as he went into a coughing spasm.

"Bein' as 'ow it's a bad night, Christmas Eve, with the snow an all, you'd think the streets would be glummed wi' birds just ready for the pickin', but a' I get is a kerchief—an' that I gave your brother. Iffen I don't come home wi' a monkey, Long Sally's liable to send me back to the street, for I'm a fortnight off on me shot, and there's others what would like me room."

Jefferson fell to coughing again, and Theodosia put her arms around him. One large tear rolled from her eye and coursed down her cheek.

" 'Ere now, lassie, Theodosia, no need to make a waterin' pot. There's three of us in the same boat now, and that's always better than one. Mayhap you've got a

few coins? Iffen I can pay me landlady—that hag Long
Sally, devil take 'er black 'eart—a little on 'count, you
can be puttin' up wi' me. It is Christmas an all, an' you
two looks like pound dealers to me—'onest, you might
say. I got me 'alf a loaf of black bread and a bit
o' cheese laid by, and maybe, it bein' Christmas, I can
fadge a bit o' stout offen the keep down the street."

Theo looked at her new friend anxiously. No matter
what, she thought, anything would be better than allowing Jefferson to die in a church. And there was
something about Riband Peg that she liked very much.
If their situations had been reversed, she thought,
doubtless she would have been very much like the
game young female who smiled kindly at her.

"I—I have a little money," Theo admitted.

"That's the billet, love!" Peg said, standing up and
shaking out her skirts. "Now, I'll just tell Long Sally
that your me cousins from—oh, one o' the shires—she
don't know ought but London speach—and you leave
it all to me."

Gratefully, Theodosia and Jefferson followed their
new friend out of the chapel.

The beetle-browed landlord of the Bird in Hand was
not used to dealing with members of that caste known
as the Quality, and as Lord Claremont towered over
him by quite two feet, he was doubly anxious to please.

"Two lads they were, my lord yes, two lads, and I
knowed they was up to no good, so's I called upon the
magistrate—Squire Elderdew, as is, my lord—but they
left the phaeton here and were off on the Mail afore we
could catch 'em."

"The London Mail?" Clare asked, barely restraining

himself from grasping the fat man by the collar of his greasy apron.

"Aye, that were it—the London Mail, it were the very one they took. I said to squire, I said—"

But Clare did not stop to hear this recital of domestic conversation. Swiftly, he turned to Sexton. "You can take the curricle back to Southcote Place! I'll go on to Town in the phaeton, if she hasn't sprung a leader! Thank God that she came this far without overturning them or breaking her neck!"

"Her?" The landlord stared after the gentleman with an extremely perplexed look on his face. Quality, he decided, was not by way of being the sort of trade he wanted in his respectable hostelry.

The section of town Riband Peg called home was known, she informed Theodosia, as Strawberry Hill, although why it should be called by that name no one knew, for nothing—not even a blade of grass—would be persuaded to grow in the soot and filth which covered the streets and the sadly rundown buildings that comprised the area.

Even as the snow fell into the open, running sewers that lined the unpaved streets, it was mingled with gray, powdery soot from the coal burning in fireplaces. At that early hour of the morning, there were few people about on the streets. And that, Theo thought, was just as well, for the thin, ragged children sitting lifelessly in the doorways were expressionless and hollow-eyed, and the few women she saw were obviously plying their trade to a largely disinterested and very rough-looking clientele. Once or twice, she and Jefferson were accosted by these gaunt, grotesque creatures who smelled of gin and dirt, but Riband Peg was quick to fend them away with a swing of her reticule and a torrent of abuse, pushing her friends on before her like two stunned children.

"Well, this 'ere is what I calls 'ome," Peg said, stopping before an ancient brick building whose glass windows had long ago been broken out and replaced with rags and sheets of board. The place where there had once been a door was empty, and sooty snow was drifting across the hallway. An empty gin bottle lay forlornly on the step, and Peg stepped over it, beckoning her friends in with her. "First I got to see Long Sally and get the key to my room. Old witch locked me out proper, she did," she said, without ill will, picking up her skirts as she entered the house.

Theodosia was almost overcome by the overwhelming stench of boiled cabbage and worse as she followed Peg up the rickety stairs, supporting Jefferson under one arm. At a door on the first landing, Peg stopped and rapped sharply. "Open up, ye old fuss-boggle, it's I, Peg!"

There was a scruffling sound, like that made by rats running across a stone floor from the other side of the door, and the judas hole shot open. "Get 'way wi' ya, trollop, lest you've got the ready," said a rough female voice, while Theo stared in fascination at the single hideously bloodshot eyeball peering from the tiny opening in the door.

"I've your blunt, you old graveworm," Peg replied. "Now open the door!"

There was the sound of several locks turning, and that command was obeyed, to reveal an ancient crone dressed all in rusty black, from the widow's cap on her yellowing, stringy locks, to the pair of men's boots into which her feet were firmly stuffed with old newspapers and rags. A face so encased in layers of fat that it bore a close resemblance to a suet pudding was the only trace of humanity about the form that shuffled back a few inches to admit them into the apartment. "Lemme see the color o' yer coin, Peg." The woman held out a ham-like hand, tightly encased in a tattered black mitt.

Theodosia stared about her in undisguised wonder. From floor to ceiling the small room was crammed with layer upon layer of used clothing. There were stacks of men's coats hanging in one corner, a pile of disreputable-looking waistcoats on a chair, and shoes of every description piled willy-nilly almost up to the upper casement of the single window. From a string hung across the rafters, petticoats, dresses, tippets, pelisses, cloaks, and other feminine fripperies, most of it sadly outdated or of a rather cheap origin, had been carelessly thrown. In a stack of boxes pushed against another wall, hats, bonnets, and caps spilled out across the dusty floor.

"Do give her the blunt!" Peg told Theodosia. Then, as the American lady dug into her pocket, she added, somewhat mendaciously, "Long Sally's by way of being a draper dealer—'mong her other lays."

"None o' yer gab, me gal!" the old crone said, her pudgy fingers wriggling at Theo, who placed a guinea into her palm. "Coo!" The old woman said, biting down on the coin with her few remaining teeth. She regarded Theo suspiciously. "And 'oo might you be, that's got golden guineas, to be goin' about wit' the likes of Peg?" She cackled. "I tol' you, Peg, that's the way to make your blunt! Look at yon Liz—she's never short her blunt!"

"Pox carry you away, you old witch," Peg snapped. "These is my cousins—from—from Australia. They was transported and they made good down there, come to see me!"

"Th-that's right," Theo said, as the old woman screwed up one eye and studied her suspiciously. "M' brother and I, we did quite well—sheep farming!"

Jefferson sneezed and nodded miserably.

The old woman bit at the coin once again, then nodded. From a chatelaine at her waist, she withdrew a purse and counted out several coins into her own hand, as if it pained her a great deal to part with them. With a sigh, she handed them to Theodosia, but Peg snatched them away and counted them out in her own hand. "Your greed will get you a stick in the back yet, you old nip-cheese! Give me the other two round-boys afore I knocks you good!"

Long Sally sighed and reluctantly produced two more shillings. "There! Never let it be said that Long Sal cheated no one!"

"Like 'ell!" Peg replied frankly. "An' I'll thank you not to be botherin' of me for more, either, cause you ain't about to get it, not until Friday!"

With a sniff and a rustle of her skirts, she shepherded her "cousins" out of the room, slamming the door behind her.

Long Sally's small eyes were riveted upon that panel. She turned the coin over in her hands. "Them's no Australians that *I* ever heard of! Peg's ma was hung at Bridewell, and 'er daddy been at Dartmoor annytime these past ten year!" She bit the coin yet again. "And that were a Yankee speech, sure as I used to work the harbor dives in Plymouth!" She chuckled, and went to fetch up an ancient black calèche bonnet of greenish-black linsey. As she tied the strings beneath one of her many chins, she chuckled to herself. "An' won't the redbreasts at Bow Street be surprised to see Long Sally there on the right side o' the law, for oncet! I'll lay this 'ere guinea there's a hundred more to be had for laying information against a couple of Yanks loose in London!"

From beneath a pile of men's smallclothes, she withdrew a bottle of gin. Uncorking it, she took a long pull. "Ahh," she sighed to herself, sitting down in the chair where the waistcoats reposed. "Perhaps just a pull or two more to get up me courage, now. A hundred guineas or more for Long Sally bein' so honest! My, my, my, don't that beat the shot!"

She cackled unpleasantly.

Riband Peg's room was sparsely furnished, with just a bed, a dresser, and a chair, but it was clean and showed signs that its occupant cherished some dreams of another life. Stuck in the cracked mirror above the dresser was an Immigration Bill advertising the bountiful life to be found for single females of marriage age in the Dominion of Canada, fare only four pounds and six, and a Rowlandson broadside sheet of a stout yeoman farmer defending England against the onslaught of Boney had been tacked to the wall above the bed.

Removing her bonnet, Peg adjured Jefferson to lie down upon the bed and pull the quilt up about himself while she put the last of her coal upon the grate. "In time, we'll have a nice cup of tea—though I've only got two mugs, so Theodosia and I will have to take turns," she said, bustling about to make her guests comfortable. "Theodosia, do you take the chair, and I'll just sit here on the rug," she said, indicating a small rag carpet spread before the hearth. "Bread and cheese and tea—not such a terrible feast at Christmas, is it? There've been times when I didn't get that much. I was put on the parish when they send my ma to the nubbing-cheat, and then, at Christmas we had a bag pudding! Oh, that were a rare treat. But they beat me, so I run away." She held up her chin. "Besides, I didn't want to go into the factory. Better to go to the gallows like me ma than be stuck in one o' them dark 'ell-'oles." She bent to stir up the coals beneath the kettle with a stick, then stood bolt upright. "Jefferson! Thomas Jefferson! 'E's president or prime minister or whatever of America, ain't 'e? You two is Yanks!" She turned to look from one Clement to the other with wonder.

"Oh, you might as well know the whole story, Peg," Theo said, "You've been good to us and—and oh, we are in the devil of a fix!" Another tear rolled down Theo's cheek, and she brushed it away angrily.

" 'Ere now, no need to waterin'-pot, Theodosia," Peg advised. "Although in the ordinary way, I do like a good cry meself. Lor', when they pressed Rob—he was my man, y'ken—they pressed 'im for sea—I cried for two weeks. We was goin' to Canada and start all over again, 'onest and pound-dealin', with a good little farm, til the press gang got 'im. But now do ye tell me your troubles, for I'm sure you've got a tale to tell!"

And so, over bread and cheese and weak black tea, Theodosia told the pickpocket most of the story of their time in England. Peg, whose experiences of the upper classes was very sharply limited, sat upon the hearthrug, her knees drawn up to her chin, her red head cradled in her hands, listening as if to a fairy tale. From time to time, however, her shrewd cockney sense asserted itself, as she asked Theodosia several sharp and very intelligent questions.

"And so, when that odious footman turned us away, we came to the church, and there we met you! And here we are, and Peg, I'm at a standstill to know what to do next!" Theo finished, nibbling on the last of the hard cheese.

Riband Peg pushed her hand through her henna'd hair. "Well, the first thing to do is try to get a message to that marquess of yours—though he sounds a bit like a rum cove to me, although you must know your own mind. Me, I don't bear the Crown no great love, not since they pressed me Rob, but that's neither 'ere nor there, for I'll sing no sad tales, but iffen I were you, I'd be wanting to go to America and marry myself to some fine and prosperous farmer, to have a couple 'ead of cattle and some sheep and some goats and field upon field of growin' things." She stood up and dusted off her skirts. "What you have to do is lay 'and on some pen and paper. And while we're a-dippin' into that pound o' yourn, mayhap we could lay in some food and some tea for that brother o' yours, for stay 'ere you shall till that marquess can come and fetch you away safe-like Theodosia!"

Peg went to the door and opened it. "Davey! Davey White!" She shouted into the hallway. "Come on up 'ere and do a service for Peg, lad!"

She turned to Theo. "Davey's Liz White's lad, and a

pound-dealin' boy for them as he trusts. It's kicks and curses 'e gets from 'is ma, but I show 'im a bit o' kindness now and then when I 'ave the ready, and 'e's willing to show me a turn or two." She sighed moodily. "If me Rob 'adn't been pressed, and we'd a gotten buckled, I'd 'ave a kid 'is age by now, I suppose."

In a very short time, a dirty-faced urchin appeared in the room. Peg handed him several shillings of Theo's money. "Now, lovey, I want you to run and fetch paper and pen and ink for me cousin from Australia 'ere—'is brother's by way of bein' sick, and 'e's got to send a note round to a man on Grosvenor Square. D'you think you can carry it?"

"Coo! Wid' all the swells?" the little boy asked.

"Aye," Peg nodded. "M'cousin's goin' into service there, see, as soon's 'e's on 'is feet again, but 'e's got to let the gentleman know 'e's delayed, else 'e'll loose 'is place. There's a sixpence in it for you, lovey."

"Sixpence! I be back in a flash, Peg!" the lad promised, darting away.

And he was as good as his word. The pen he provided was sadly dull, the paper of a very inferior quality, and the ink thick with age, but Theo seized upon it as if it were manna from heaven.

> *Dear Albert,* [she wrote]
> *I am in Desperate Trouble, through a set of Circumstances too complex to relate here, but we have been Forced to Flee Southcote Place under threat of Devonshire Prison, but sought to gain admittance to your house, but were Turned Away. A very kind Lady by the name of Riband Peg has offered us*

*Shelter at this address, but Jeff. is terribly
ill, and I beg you to come and fetch us away
as soon as you may. I have decided to Accept your Kind Addresses, and shall en-
deavor to make you a good Wife.*

Yours and etc.

THEODOSIA CLEMENT

Reading this over, Theodosia decided that it would
have to do. Since there was no sealing wax to be had,
she folded it up and handed it to the boy. "Please be
certain that Lord Torville receives this," she said, "and
I will be certain that he shall make you a handsome reward when he comes to fetch me and my brother away.
A guinea!"

The boy's eyes widened. "A coachwheel! Lumme, I
ain't never even *seen* a coachwheel!" he said, taking
the letter from her hands and dashing out the door.

"Well, now that that's settled," Peg said, "let me see
what I may do about putting us up some dinner of
some sort. Are you sure you wouldn't like to be in
some skirts again, Theodosia?"

Thinking upon Riband Peg's tastes with some hesita-
tion, Theo shook her head. "No! It—it is such a nov-
elty to be in trousers that I think I would like to keep
my disguise a bit longer. Let me look to my brother,
Peg."

"Good cup of tea and 'e'll be right as trivet in no
time," that hearty female promised. "Say, Theo, would
ye like to learn the trick o' my trade? Rob used to say,
ye know, that you ought to know a bit about every lay,
for there's no tellin' when ye'll be in a pinch, like." She
sighed. "Poor Rob, I wonder upon 'im. . . ."

The snow had abated by tea time, and the street sweepers were already hard at work in Grosvenor Square when Lord Claremont's phaeton drew up before number fourteen.

Clare jumped down from the perch and ran up the shallow steps, rapping loudly upon the door. He was admitted by the same minion who had earlier turned away the Clements. If Theo had been able to see the way in which Clare thrust that person aside with a snarl and proceeded up the steps to the marquess's study, she would have felt amply revenged.

Clare found Torville seated in a comfortable chair by the fire, wrapped in his dressing gown, an elaborate affair of silk-embroidered dragons with a great deal of gold braid. As Clare burst in the room, the picture of outrage, the marquess lazily lowered his evening paper and picked up the glass of very fine brandy from the table at his side.

"Where is she?" Clare demanded, striding across the room and standing over the smaller man, his driving whip still clutched in his hand.

Torville raised one brow. "I say, Southcote, that coat ain't at all the thing. Weston, isn't it? Scott, dear fellow—always Scott for a driving coat."

"Steyland!" Clare thundered.

The marquess sighed. "I presume, Southcote, that you mean Miss Clement—and her hapless brother. And I also presume that you have driven from Devon in the devil's own hurry, and have not stopped at Southcote House, but have come directly here."

"Where is Theodosia?" Clare repeated, enraged by Torville's calm.

The marquess folded his paper. "If you had stopped at Upper Mount Street, Southcote, you would have found the billet I sent round to you, telling you Peerless Theo's direction." He held his glass up to the fire, examining the color of the wine. "I would offer you a glass, but I imagine you would prefer to rescue Miss Clement before anything else. I had the opportunity, you understand, and dear boy, if it had been any other female but Theo, believe me, I should have instantly gone to her rescue. But, dear Southcote, when you have known Theo as long as I have, you will learn that she is perfectly capable of rescuing herself from any scrape. But I thought that I should offer the better man the opportunity." He suddenly leveled his cool gaze upon Clare. "I may wish you to the devil, Southcote, but it's you she's set her heart upon, and I am, I hope, a good enough loser to bow out of the game when I know I've been defeated."

For the first time in his life, Clare was speechless with astonishment.

"What she sees in you, I'll never understand," the marquess continued, reaching into his robe and handing Clare a folded piece of rough paper. "But doubtless I shall have my revenge by watching her lead you through the devil's chase. In that aspect, at least, you two are matched well, Southcote! But I warn you, this is the last time you'll have any help from me, dear boy. If ever she should apply to me again, I will not wait for you to arrive, repentant and out of breath. She is Peerless Theodosia, Southcote—treat her well, with a light hand on the bridle!"

Clare opened the note and scanned Theo's agitated handwriting. His brows drew together. "I see," he said quietly, and thrust out his hand to his rival.

Torville looked at it for a second, then, with a small shrug, grasped it firmly. "I wish you luck, old man, but remember what I said! Easy on the bridle!"

These last words were thrown at Lord Claremont's retreating back.

The marquess settled back in his chair again and picked up his paper. There was the faintest trace of an amused smile on his lips.

It took Clare rather longer to find the address Theo had given than he expected, for Strawberry Hill was not a section of London which had previously enjoyed his patronage. By stopping several times to inquire the way, he was eventually led to Byng Street, and the appalling condition of this neighborhood did little to reassure him.

Several times he was accosted by a set of females whom he could only castigate as "Covent Garden nuns," and more than once he found it necessary to threaten away rough-looking men with his coachwhip and an offer to give them a taste of the home-brewed, if they cared to try, and he was suddenly very glad that Theodosia had availed herself of one of his pistols.

But when he finally drew up before the house occupied by Riband Peg, his heart sank into his boots, for there was a large crowd milling about the doorway and several armed and red-waistcoated men passing in and out of the doorway.

Fortunately the crowd's interest was totally enveloped in the goings-on at 34 Byng Street, else the arrival upon the scene of a well-breeched swell with a bang-up phaeton and pair might have aroused more hostility than even Lord Claremont was prepared to deal with.

Jumping down from the perch, he shouldered his way past several tawdry-looking females passing a bottle amongst themselves and clasped one of the uniformed men, whom he recognized by his waistcoat as a Bow Street runner, on the shoulder. "What's going on?" he demanded.

The man was about to give him a hasty reply when he recognized someone in authority. "Lord Claremont Southcote, Foreign Office," Clare said helpfully.

The man wiped his nose on the sleeve of his coat. "Well, my lord, it's about time," he said indignantly. "There's a couple o' Yank spies up there, a-'oldin' of a gal an' one of our men 'ostage, wid a great popper, an' it's a rare pickle we're all in, sir, seein' as 'ow they won't come out and we can't go in wit'out takin inno-cent lives, and this crowd a-turnin' mean, 'avin' no great love of redbreasts, if you get my drift."

"Good God!" Clare muttered, pushing his way through the crowd and into the house.

"Make way! Make way! 'E's from the Foreign Office an' come to smooth things out!" the runner cried, following close upon his heels.

In the hallway, Clare was accosted by an enormous bag of a female dressed all in black and reeking heavily of spirits. "It was I as laid the information 'gainst them Yank spies! Jonathans in our midst!" she said proudly, dropping one greasy eyelid over a small, beady eye. She clutched at Clare's arm with fat, swollen fingers.

215

"Tell me, is there a reward in this for a-peachin' on such a pair?"

Clare, repulsed, pushed her away and ran up the stairs. On the top landing, he found a group of runners standing uncertainly around a door. The leader, a kindly-looking Irishman of middle age, was talking to that firmly closed portal. "Now, see 'ere, you've got to come out at some time, y'know!" he was pleading.

"Mr. O'Malley, this 'ere gentleman's from the Foreign Office," the first runner said, huffing slight from the steep ascent.

"Why should we come out?" asked a familar voice from inside. "We've got food and tea and even a bottle of wine."

O'Malley mopped at his brow and turned to Clare. "It's glad enough I am to see you, my lord. We've been a-talkin' and a-talkin' till we're blue in the face, but listen to reason they will not. One man we sent along, Hornby, and them Jonathans is a holdin' him hostage, along with a gal, and come out they will not. Says they mean to shoot if we tries anything!"

Clare moved to the door and rapped sharply. "Theo—Theo, let me in!" he commanded.

There was silence on the other side, then a shuffling noise.

"Lord Claremont?" Theodosia's voice asked. "Is that *you?*"

"Theodosia Clement, open this door, or I shall break it down over your head!" Clare shouted.

"Where is Torville?" Theo asked.

"I've been there. He left it to me to rescue you. Theo—I—well, damme, Theo, open this door so I can talk to you, man to—to woman!"

"Don't ye do it," said a strong cockney voice. " 'E'll have you in Devonshire Prison for sure!"

There was a brief silence.

Theo giggled. "Lord Claremont, will you promise that Jeff and I will not go to Devonshire Prison if I allow you to come in?" she asked. "And promise that you will not be angry with me for stealing your phaeton and your pistols?"

"Theo—Miss Clement—Theodosia! I would rather see you steal a hundred phaetons than be in Devonshire Prison! It—it was merely a figure of speech!" Clare took a deep breath. "Miss Clement—Theodosia—I'm sorry. I—damme, a man can't tell a female he loves her with all of Bow Street looking on!"

There was a long silence on the other side of the door.

"Make 'im say it again!" the cockney voice finally said. "Proper now, too, Theodosia!"

"You heard what Peg said—Clare?" Theo asked.

"Theo Clement, open this door!" Lord Claremont shouted, rattling the knob.

"Not until you repeat that last statement, my lord," Miss Clement said firmly.

Clare pushed his fingers through his hair. "All right, damn your eyes, you she-devil! Miss Clement, I love you! I want you to marry me! Theo, now open the door so that I may give you a proper kiss!"

"Is that 'ow the toffs do it?" asked the cockney voice, rather disappointed. "Iffen I was you, I'd have the marquess. 'E'd get down on his knees and say it all proper, like they do at the theater."

"But Lord Claremont will be an earl, you know," Theo replied. "Don't you think that's almost as good?"

"Theo!"

The door opened a crack, and Lord Claremont Southcote found himself staring down the barrel of his own dueling pistol. Uneasily, he edged his way into the room.

Theo slammed the door behind him. For a few seconds, they stared at one another, the man in the stained driving coat and the female in men's breeches and shirt. Then, without a word, Theodosia fell into Clare's arms, relaxing against his chest with a sigh while he held her very tightly, rocking her back and forth in his arms like a child. "Oh, Clare, thank God, it is you and not Albert," she murmured, while he stroked at her hacked-off curls with tender fingers. Suddenly, she pulled back and looked at him. "But what about Miss Morton-West, Clare?"

He pulled her to him again with a fierce embrace. "Edwina has cried off, once she had a taste of my foul temper. I think that she and Lieutenant Steyland intend to make a match of it."

Theo giggled again. "You did mean it, did you not? That you love me, I mean, and that you want to—to marry me."

"I was never more serious about anything in my life! When I lost my twin, I thought I had lost a half of myself. But—knowing you, being with you, Theo, I know now that I have just discovered my true half! My dearest love, I have been evil-tempered and tyrannical and—detestably high-handed. And I shall doubtless continue to be! Can you accept that?"

"But Clare, I have been roguish and—and fast, and always in and out of scrapes! And I shall probably always be so! Can you deal with me that way?"

"I think we shall contrive, you and I. At least it will never be dull!"

Lord Claremont Southcote put his hand beneath Miss Clement's chin to lift her face to his, when Jefferson fell into a sneezing fit again. She pressed his hand with a speaking look and drew away. "Oh, Jeff has a terrible cold, but I think he will be all right. Lord Claremont Southcote, may I present Miss Margaret Goode, also known as Riband Peg, who has been very kind to us, and has taught me all about picking pockets, and Mr. Homby, of Bow Street—I am quite glad that you are here, Clare, for we are in desperate need of a fourth to play deep basset, which is the only card game we all know—" Theo gestured airily about the room with her pistol.

For the first time, Lord Claremont became aware of the presence of other persons in this small chamber. He looked from Riband Peg, who was sizing him up most uncomfortably, to a short, pleasant-faced man in the scarlet waistcoat of a runner, to Jefferson, seated in the bed with a handkerchief pressed against his nose. He bowed to Peg and to Mr. Homby, and produced his own handkerchief for Jefferson.

"I suppose, since we are to be related, we should try to make the best of it, Jeff! Forgive me!"

Jefferson sneezed, waving him away. "I told Theo if she wanted you, she'd have to keep you in England, for all of me. But mind you make her happy, my lord!'

"I shall try," Clare promised gravely.

"I 'ope you know how to play deep basset," Mr. Homby inquired, shuffling a deck of greasy playing cards. "It's a favorite game of the wife and m'self! Miss Clement 'ere's a capital player, for a Yankee."

219

"Oh, Clare! Can you get a man out of the Navy? Peg's beau was pressed aboard the *Lighthawk* on the eve of their wedding and I have convinced her that you can have him freed. And then she intends to give up the *diving lay*—that's picking pockets!—and emigrate to America with him. They mean to go to Ohio and have a farm and lots of babies and—Clare, please say you can get Rob released!"

Lord Claremont's arm tightened about his beloved's waist as Peg's hopeful eyes gazed up at him. His lips twitched. "If you promise not to teach my wife anything more about the—er—*diving lay*, I think that I might be able to contrive forms of release!" he said.

"Oh, my lord!" Peg said in raptures. "That would be above all things! Can you really do so? Theodosia says you are a very powerful sort of flash cove, and knows all the high-up toffs!"

"It will be my wedding present to my wife," Clare promised. "Because you have been good enough to protect her from the consequences of her own—from my folly!" he amended swiftly, grasping Theo's fingers in his own as they stole across his waistcoat toward his pocket watch.

" 'Ere now, you don't go a pluckin' of a downy one," Peg admonished. "Oh, to think I shall have me Rob back to me, when I never expected to see 'im ever again!"

"Mr. Homby, I do not know what I shall do for you, seeing what—er—inconvenience Miss Clement has put you through," Clare said to the runner.

The little man shrugged. "Well, now, it's all in a day's work, you might say! Though you could imagine me shock, my lord, when I discovered these 'ere Yank spies was no more nor a schoolboy an a gal! And no more spies than you nor I, and so I shall tell the chief, do you straighten this all out." He winked. "Actually, all in all, it ain't been bad. Miss Clement 'ere is as entertainin' as a play, she is!"

He took a sip from his glass. "Course, things will 'ave to be straightened out a bit—but no doubt you can see to that, my lord. Violatin' parole's a serious matter, from what I understand. That ain't in our line so much, you know, but now that you're 'ere, you can fix it all!"

"The devil!" Lord Claremont murmured. "Not my department at all."

"Clare—do you mean that Jeff and I shall have to go to prison after all?" Theo asked, trembling.

He ran a hand through his hair. "I think we may have to think a bit—but I'm sure we can do something!"

There was more pounding upon the door, and Theodosia spun about, the pistol leveled at the paneling.

"Clare! I say, Clare, you are in there!"

"Theodosia! Jefferson! Open this door at once! At once, I say!"

"It's my father!" Clare said in tones of wonder.

"And mine!" Theo exclaimed, dropping the gun on the floor and throwing open the portals.

The Earl of Southcote, looking rather bored, entered the room, followed by a tall gentleman whose marked resemblance to the Clements proclaimed him to be none other than Senator Thaddeus Clement.

"Father!" cried Theodosia, throwing herself into his arms.

The Earl of Southcote, a less demonstrative man, removed his snuffbox from his pocket and lifted a pinch of his mixture to his nostrils, surveying the company with a jaundiced eye.

"Sharper than a serpent's tooth and all that," he remarked absently. "Can't see what all this fuss is about, Clare! War's over! Signed a treaty with the Americans, just last week, matter of fact—and came home again, only to find that you'd made a damned mess of things. Sent all those people away—never could abide runners. Or slum dweller either, for that manner. What sort of an establishment is this to be bringing Thaddeus's brats to, eh?"

"The war's over, my lord?" Clare repeated.

"Just told you that, didn't I? Is that Thaddeus's daughter? No—can't be. Little Theodosia looked like her ma. Now you, lad, in the bed, you're—ah—Jefferson, ain't it? You look like your father. Ah—that must be Thaddeus's daughter huggin' 'im, but what's she doing dressed up like a man, hey?"

"My lord, I shall contrive to explain it all to you later. But first, allow me to introduce you to Miss—ah—Riband Peg, and Mr. Homby of Bow Street."

"Ha," the Earl said laconically.

"And the lady hugging Mr. Clement, sir, is Miss Theodosia Clement. Theodosia, will you not introduce me to my prospective father-in-law?"

Theo turned from her father. "Oh, Father—this is the earl's son—Clare—Lord Claremont Southcote. He wanted to put Jeff and me into Devonshire Prison, but now we are to be married—I assure you, Father, that I am excessively fond of him, and I think that we shall suit very well."

Mr. Clement surveyed Clare. "Devonshire Prison?

222

Marriage? Lord Southcote, what's this all about, do you know?"

"I haven't the faintest idea, old boy," the earl replied. "But now that we've managed to capture all of them in one place, I dare say we ought to repair back to my house. Chef's a Frenchman, gets a little put out if dinner's kept waitin'. And that butler of mine is liable to decant the port!"

"Decant the port! Decant the port! Lord Southcote, my friend," said Mr. Clement awfully, "that, my lord, that would be sin against a good bottle of wine! Well, it seems as if my daughter wants to marry your son. Any objections? If Theo's suited, I'm suited. She's always known her own mind."

Lord Southcote looked Theodosia over from head to toe. "Well, she beats that pudding-faced female he had on string last time I saw him, say what? But dashed strange, gal, to be runnin' about the slums of London in men's clothes, or is that the latest fashion? Go out of the country, can't keep up with these things. Looks like one of those dashed notions that female Talleyrand had in keeping might take into her head."

Clement shrugged. "I'm sure Theo has a good reason. She always does. Well, Jefferson, my boy, you look a trifle peaked. Better come on now with us, and see that his lordship's doctor has a look at you."

"I think I shall just run along, then," Mr. Homby said, "now that everything's settled right and tight." He placed his hat upon his head and bowed to Theo. "Well, miss, you've given me a story to tell the wife, and no doubt!"

"Father—will you be so good as to take Peg along with you? She is a particular friend of mine, and I—I wish to keep her by me until a certain gentleman in the navy is mustered out," Theo called to her father.

"But what about my clothes?" Peg asked.

"You and Theo shall go out tomorrow and buy a whole new wardrobe, Peg—only give us a moment of privacy," Clare pleaded, putting an arm about Miss Clement.

Riband Peg nodded. "Then it's glad enough I am to leave this room and everything in it—provided I'll have my Rob back to me again!"

She and Jefferson followed the others down the stairs.

Lord Claremont Southcote regarded Miss Clement. Miss Clement regarded Lord Claremont. "Hoyden," he said fondly, taking her into his arms.

"Tyrant," she sighed happily, lifting her face to receive his kiss.